Enid Blyton

The Mystery of
the Burnt Cottage

D1356684

Also by Enid Blyton in Dean

Enid Blyton

The Mystery of
the Burnt Cottage

DEAN

Blyton, Enid

Mystery of the
burnt cottage /
Enid Blyton
JF

1828614

First published in Great Britain 1943
Reissued 2004 by Dean
an imprint of Egmont UK Limited
239 Kensington High Street, London W8 6SA

ISBN 978 0 6035 6162 7
ISBN 0 6035 6162 4

Printed and bound in Singapore

1 3 5 7 9 10 8 6 4 2

Contents

Contents

1. THE BURNING COTTAGE

It was at half past nine on a dark April night that all the excitement began.

The village of Peterswood was perfectly quiet and peaceful, except for a dog barking somewhere. Then suddenly, to the west of the village, a great light flared up.

Larry Daykin was just getting into bed when he saw it. He had pulled back his curtains so that the daylight would wake him, and he suddenly saw the flare to the west.

'Golly! What's that?' he said. He called to his sister. 'Daisy! I say, come here and look. There's a funny flare-up down in the village somewhere.'

His sister came into the bedroom in her nightdress. She looked out of the window.

'It's a fire!' she said. 'It looks pretty big, doesn't it? I wonder what it is. Do you think it's someone's house on fire?'

'We'd better go and see,' said Larry, excited. 'Let's get dressed again. Mummy and Daddy are busy, so they won't know anything about the fire. Come on, hurry.'

Larry and Daisy dressed quickly, and then ran down the stairs and out into the dark garden. As they went down the lane they passed another house, and heard the sound of hurrying footsteps coming down the drive there.

'It's Pip, I bet!' said Larry, and shone his torch up the drive. The light picked out a boy about his own age, and with him a small girl of about eight.

'Hello, Bets! You coming too?' called Daisy, surprised. 'I should have thought you'd have been asleep.'

'Larry!' called Pip. 'It's a fire, isn't it? Whose house is burning, do you think? Will they send for the fire engine?'

'The house will be burnt down before the firemen come all the way from the next village!' said Larry. 'Come on – it looks as if it's down Haycock Lane.'

They all ran on together. Some of the villagers had seen the glare too, and were running down the lane as well. It was exciting.

'It's Mr Hick's house,' said a man. 'Sure as anything it's his house.'

They all poured down to the end of the lane. The glare became higher and brighter.

'It's not the house!' cried Larry, 'It's the cottage he works in, in the garden – his workroom. Golly, there won't be much left of it!'

There certainly wouldn't. The place was old, half-timbered and thatched, and the dry straw of the roof was blazing strongly.

Mr Goon, the village policeman, was there, directing men to throw water on the flames. He saw the children and shouted at them.

'Clear orf, you! Clear orf!'

'That's what he always says to children,' said Bets. 'I've never heard him say anything else.'

It was not the least use throwing pails of water on the flames. The policeman yelled for the chauffeur.

'Where's Mr Thomas? Tell him to get out the hosepipe he uses to clean the car.'

'Mr Thomas has gone to fetch the master,' shouted a woman's voice. 'He's gone to the station to meet the London train!'

It was Mrs Minns, the cook, speaking. She was a comfortable-looking person, who was in a very scared state now. She filled pails of water from a tap, her hands trembling.

'It's no use,' said one of the villagers. 'Can't stop this fire now. It's got too big a hold.'

'Someone's phoned for the fire engine,' said another man. 'But by the time it gets here the whole place will be gone.'

'Well, there's no fear of the house catching,' said the policeman. 'Wind's in the opposite direction luckily. My word, what a shock for Mr Hick when he comes home.'

The four children watched everything with excitement. 'It's a shame to see such a nice little cottage go up in flames,' said Larry. 'I wish they'd let us do something – throw water, for instance.'

A boy about the same size as Larry ran up with a pail of water and threw it towards the flames, but his aim was bad, and some of it went over Larry. He shouted at the boy, 'Hey, you! Some of that went over me! Look what you're doing, for goodness' sake!'

'Sorry, old boy,' said the boy, in a funny drawling sort of voice. The flames shot up and lit the whole garden well. Larry saw that the boy was plump, well-dressed and rather pleased with himself.

'He's the boy who has come to live with his father and mother in the hotel opposite,' said Pip in a low voice to Larry. 'He's awful. Thinks he knows everything, and has so much pocket money he doesn't know what to do with it!'

The policeman saw the boy carrying the pail. 'Here you!' he yelled. 'Clear orf! We don't want children getting in the way.'

'I am not a child,' said the boy indignantly. 'Can't you see I'm helping?'

'You clear orf!' said Mr Goon.

A dog suddenly appeared and barked round the policeman's ankles in a most annoying way. Mr Goon was angry. He kicked out at the dog.

'This your dog?' he called to the boy. 'Call him orf!'

The boy took no notice but went to get another pail of water. The dog had a wonderful time round Mr Goon's trousered ankles.

'Clear orf!' said the policeman, kicking out again. Larry and the others chuckled. The dog was a nice little thing, a black Scottie, very nimble on his short legs.

'He belongs to that boy,' said Pip. 'He's a topping dog, absolutely full of fun. I wish he was mine.'

A shower of sparks flew up into the air as part of the straw roof fell in. There was a horrible smell of burning and smoke. The children moved back a little.

There came the sound of a car down the lane. A shout went up. 'Here's Mr Hick!'

The car drew up in the drive by the house. A man got out and ran down the garden to where the burning cottage stood.

'Mr Hick, sir, sorry to say your workroom is almost destroyed,' said the policeman. 'Did our best to save it, sir, but the fire got too big a hold. Any idea what caused the fire, sir?'

'How am I to know?' said Mr Hick impatiently. 'I've only just got back from the London train. Why wasn't the fire engine sent for?'

'Well, sir, you know it's in the next town,' said Mr Goon, 'and by the time we knew of the fire, the flames were already shooting through the roof. Do you happen to know if you had a fire in the grate this morning, sir?'

'Yes, I did,' said Mr Hick. 'I was working here early this morning, and I had kept the fire in all night. I was burning wood, and I dare say that after I left a spark flew out and set light to something. It may have smouldered all afternoon without any one knowing. Where's Mrs Minns, my cook?'

'Here, sir,' said poor trembling Mrs Minns. 'Oh, sir, this is a terrible thing, sir! You never like me to go into your work-cottage, sir, so I didn't go in, or I might have seen that a fire was starting!'

'The door was locked,' said the policeman. 'I tried it myself, before the flames got round to it. Well – there goes the last of your cottage, sir!'

There was a crash as the half-timbered walls fell in. The flames rose high, and everyone stepped back, for the heat was terrific.

Then Mr Hick suddenly seemed to go mad. He caught hold of the policeman's arm and shook it hard. 'My papers!' he said, in a shaking voice. 'My precious old documents! They were in there! Get them out, get them out!'

'Now, sir, be reasonable,' said Mr Goon, looking at the furnace not far from him. 'No one can save anything at all – they couldn't from the beginning.'

'My PAPERS!' yelled Mr Hick, and made a dart towards the burning workroom, as if he meant to search in the flames. Two or three people pulled him back.

'Now, sir, now, sir, don't do anything silly,' said the policeman anxiously. 'Were they very valuable papers, sir?'

'Can't be replaced!' moaned Mr Hick. 'They are worth thousands of pounds to me!'

'Hope they're insured, sir,' said a man near by.

Mr Hick turned to him wildly. 'Yes – yes, they're insured – but money won't repay me for losing them!'

Bets did not know what being insured was. Larry told her quickly. 'If you have anything valuable that you are afraid might be stolen or burnt, you pay a small sum of money to an insurance company each year – and then if it does happen to be destroyed, the company will pay you the whole cost of your valuable belongings.'

'I see,' said Bets. She stared at Mr Hick. He still

seemed very upset indeed. She thought he was a funny looking man.

He was tall and stooping, and had a tuft of hair that stuck out in front. He had a long nose, and eyes hidden behind big spectacles. Bets didn't much like him.

'Clear all these people away,' said Mr Hick, looking at the villagers and the children. 'I don't want my garden trampled down all night long. There's nothing any one can do now.'

'Right, sir,' said Mr Goon, pleased at being able to 'clear orf' so many people at once. He began to walk towards the watching people.

'Clear orf,' he said. 'Nothing to be done now. Clear orf, you children. Clear orf, everyone.'

The flames of the cottage were burning low now. The fire would burn itself out, and that would be the end. The children suddenly felt sleepy after their excitement, and their eyes smarted with the smoke.

'Pooh! My clothes do smell of smoke,' said Larry, disgusted. 'Come on – let's get back home. I wonder if Mummy and Daddy are looking for us.'

Larry and Daisy walked up the lane with Pip and Bets. Behind them, whistling, walked the boy with the dog. He caught them up.

'That was a real thrill, wasn't it?' he said. 'Good thing no one was hurt. I say, what about meeting tomorrow, having a game or something? I'll be in the hotel opposite Mr Hick's garden – my mother and father will be out playing golf.'

'Well –' said Larry, who didn't particularly like the look of the boy, 'Well – if we are anywhere about, we'll pick you up.'

'Right,' said the boy. 'Come on, Buster. Home, boy!'

The little Scottie, who had been circling round the children's legs, ran to the boy. They disappeared into the darkness.

'Conceited creature!' said Daisy, speaking of the boy. 'Why should he think we want to know him? I say, let's all meet in your drive tomorrow, Pip, and go down to see what's left of the cottage, shall we?'

'Right,' said Pip, turning in at his drive with Bets. 'Come on, Bets. I believe you are nearly asleep!'

Larry and Daisy went on up the lane to

their own home. They yawned. 'Poor Mr Hick!' said Daisy. 'Wasn't he upset about his precious old papers!'

2. THE FIVE FIND-OUTERS – AND DOG

The next day Larry and Daisy went to see if Pip and Bets were anywhere about. They could hear them playing in the garden and they shouted to them.

'Pip! Bets! We're here!'

Pip appeared, followed by the much smaller Bets, panting behind him.

'Seen the burnt-up cottage this morning?' asked Larry.

'Yes. And I say, what do you think – they say somebody burnt it down on purpose – that it wasn't an accident after all!' said Pip, excited.

'On *purpose*!' said Larry and Daisy. 'But whoever would do a thing like that!'

'Don't know,' said Pip. 'I overheard somebody talking about it. They said that the insurance people had been down already, and some fire expert they brought with them said that petrol had been used to start up the fire. They've got some way of finding out these things, you know.'

'Golly!' said Larry. 'But who would do it? Somebody that didn't like Mr Hick, I suppose?'

'Yes,' said Pip. 'I bet old Clear-Orf is excited to have a real crime to find out about. But he's so stupid he'll never find out a thing!'

'Look – there's that dog again,' said Bets, pointing to the little black Scottie appearing in the garden. He stood sturdily on his squat legs, his ears cocked, looking up at them as if to say 'Mind me being here?'

'Hello, Buster!' said Larry, bending down and patting his knee to make the dog come to him. 'You're a nice dog, you are. I wish you were mine. Daisy and I have never had a dog.'

'Nor have I,' said Pip. 'Here, Buster! Bone, Buster? Biscuit, Buster?'

'Woof,' said Buster, in a surprisingly deep voice for such a small dog.

'You must get him a bone *and* a biscuit,' said Bets. 'He's trusting you and believing you, Pip. Go and get them for him.'

Pip went off, with the squat little Scottie trotting beside him trustingly.

Soon they were back, Buster carrying a bone and a big biscuit in his mouth. He set them down on the ground and looked inquiringly at Pip.

'Yes, they're for you, old chap,' said Pip. 'He's not a bit of a greedy dog, is he? He waits to be told before he begins!'

Buster crunched up the bone and then swallowed the biscuit. They seemed to fill him with joy and he began to caper round and about the children, inviting them to chase him. They all thought him a wonderful little dog.

'It's a pity he has such a silly master,' said Larry. Everyone giggled. Just as they were chuckling, they heard the sound of footsteps and saw Buster's master coming to join them.

'Hello,' he said. 'I thought I heard you playing with Buster. Buster, what do you mean by running off like that! Come here!'

Buster bounced over to him in delight. It was quite plain that he adored the plump boy who owned him.

'Heard the news?' asked the boy, patting Buster. 'About someone having set fire to that workroom on purpose?'

'Yes,' said Larry. 'Pip told us. Do you believe it?'

'Rather!' said the boy. 'As a matter of fact, I suspected it before anyone else did.'

'Fibber!' said Larry at once, knowing by the conceited tone of the boy's voice that he hadn't suspected anything of the sort.

'Well, look here,' said the boy. 'I've been staying in the hotel opposite Mr Hick's garden – and last evening I saw a tramp wandering about there! I bet he did it!'

The others stared at him. 'Why should he do it?' asked Pip at last. 'Tramps don't go in and pour petrol over things and set them on fire just for fun.'

'Well,' said the boy, thinking hard, 'this tramp may have had a spite against Mr Hick. You can't tell. Mr Hick hasn't got a very good name about here for being good-tempered. He may have kicked the old tramp out of the place, or something, that very morning!'

The others thought about this. 'Let's go into the summerhouse and talk,' said Pip, feeling excited. 'This is a sort of mystery, and it would be fun if we could help to solve it.'

The boy with Buster walked into the

summerhouse too, without being asked. Buster scrambled on to Larry's knee. Larry looked pleased.

'What time did you see the tramp?' asked Pip.

'About six o'clock,' said the boy. 'A dirty old fellow he was too, in a torn mackintosh, and a frightful old hat. He was skulking along the hedge. Buster saw him and tore out, barking.'

'Did you notice if he had a tin of petrol in his hand?' asked Larry.

'No, he hadn't,' said the boy. 'He'd got a stick of some sort. That's all.'

'I say,' said Daisy suddenly. 'I say! I've got an idea!'

They all looked at her. Daisy was a great one for ideas, and usually she had good ones.

'What's the idea this time?' asked Larry.

'We'll be detectives!' said Daisy. 'We'll set ourselves to find out *who burnt the cottage.*'

'What's a detective?' asked eight year old Bets.

'It's somebody who solves a mystery,' said Larry. 'Somebody who finds out who does a crime.'

'Oh, a find-outer,' said Bets. 'I'd love to be that. I'm sure I would make a very good find-outer.'

'No, you're too little,' said Pip. Bets looked ready to cry.

'We three older ones will be proper detectives,' said Larry, his eyes shining. 'Pip, Daisy and me – the Three Great Detectives!'

'Can't I belong?' said the fat boy at once. 'I've got plenty of brains.'

The others looked at him doubtfully. His brains didn't show in his face, anyway.

'Well, we don't know you,' said Larry.

'My name is Frederick Algernon Trotteville,' said the boy. 'What are your names?'

'Mine is Laurence Daykin,' said Larry, 'and I'm thirteen.'

'Mine's Margaret Daykin, and I'm twelve,' said Daisy.

'I'm Philip Hilton, aged twelve, and this is Elizabeth, my baby sister,' said Pip.

The boy stared at them. 'You're none of you called by your names, are you?' he said. 'Larry for Laurence, Pip for Philip, Daisy for Margaret and Bets for Elizabeth. I'm always called Frederick.'

For some reason this seemed funny to the others. The boy spoke in a drawling, affected kind of voice, and somehow the name of Frederick Algernon Trotteville just seemed to suit him.

'F for Frederick, A for Algernon, T for Trotteville,' said Pip suddenly, with a grin. 'F–A–T; it could be a nickname!'

Frederick Algernon Trotteville looked rather cross at first, then he gave a grin.

'Your parents ought to have known better than to give you three names whose initials spelt "fat",' said Daisy. 'Poor old Fatty!'

Frederick Algernon sighed. He knew quite well that from now on he would be Fatty. He gazed at the little company of four friends.

'Can I belong to the detective club?' he asked. 'After all, I did tell you about a tramp.'

'It isn't a club,' said Larry. 'It's just us three older ones banding together to solve a mystery.'

'And me too!' cried Bets. 'Oh, do say I can too! You're not to leave me out!'

'Don't leave her out,' said Fatty unexpectedly. 'She's only little, but she might be some use. And I think Buster ought to belong too. He might be awfully good at smelling out hidden things.'

'What hidden things?' said Larry.

'Oh, I don't know,' said Fatty vaguely. 'You simply never know what you are going to find when you begin to solve a mystery.'

'Oh, let's all belong, Fatty and Buster too. Please!' cried Bets. Buster felt the excitement and began to whine a little, pawing at Larry with a small black foot.

The three bigger ones felt much more inclined to let Fatty join them once they realised that Buster could come too. For Buster's sake they were willing to have Fatty, conceited and the rest. Buster could be a sort of bloodhound. They felt certain that real detectives, who solved all sorts of mysteries, would have a bloodhound.

'Well,' said Larry. 'We'll all belong and try to solve the mystery of the burnt cottage.'

'We're the Five Find-Outers and Dog,' said Bets. Everyone laughed. 'What a silly name!' said Larry. But all the same, it stuck, and for the rest of those holidays, and for a very long time after, the Five Find-Outers and Dog used that name continually for themselves.

'I know all about police and detectives,' said Fatty. 'I'd better be the head of us.'

'No, you won't,' said Larry. 'I bet you don't know any more than the rest of us. And don't think that we're so stupid as not to see what a very good opinion you've got of yourself! You might as well make up your mind straightaway that we shan't believe half the tall stories you tell us! As for being head – I shall be. I always am.'

'That's right,' said Pip. 'Larry's clever. He shall be the head of the bold Find-Outers.'

'All right,' said Fatty ungraciously. 'I suppose it's four against one. Blow – is that half past twelve, – yes, it is. I must go.'

'Meet here this afternoon sharp at two,' said Larry. 'We will discuss the finding of clues then.'

'Glues?' said Bets, not hearing the word properly. 'Oh, that sounds exciting. Are glues sticky?'

'Idiot,' said Pip. 'What use you are going to be in the Find-Outers, I simply can't imagine!'

3. THE FIRST MEETING

At two o'clock sharp the Five Find-Outers and Dog met together in Pip's big garden. Pip was waiting for them, and he led them to the old summer-house.

'This had better be our headquarters,' he said. 'We shall keep wanting to meet and discuss things, I expect. It's a good place for that because it's at the bottom of the garden, and nobody can overhear us.'

They all sat down on the wooden bench that ran round the old summerhouse. Buster jumped up on to Larry's knee. Larry liked that. Fatty didn't seem to mind.

'Now,' said Larry, 'as I'm the head of us I'd better start things going. I'll just go over what we all know, and then we'll discuss what we should do.'

'I do think this is exciting,' said Bets, who was very much enjoying being one of the big ones.

'Don't interrupt, Bets,' said Pip. Bets made her face solemn and sat still and straight.

'Well, we all know that Mr Hick's cottage work-room, which stands at the end of his garden, was burnt down last night,' said Larry. 'Mr Hick was not there till the end, because his chauffeur had gone to meet him off the London train. The insurance people say that petrol was used to start the fire, so some one must have done it on purpose. The Find-Outers have made up their minds that they will find out who has done this crime. Is that right?'

'Quite right, and very well put,' said Pip, at once. Buster wagged his tail hard. Fatty opened his mouth and began to speak in his high, affected voice. 'Well, I suggest that the first thing we do is to . . .'

But Larry interrupted him at once. 'I'm doing the talking, Fatty, not you,' he said. 'Shut up!'

Fatty shut up, but he didn't look at all pleased about it. He put on a bored expression and rattled the money in his pocket.

'Now what we must do to find out who did the crime, is to discover who, if anyone, was near the workroom or in the garden that evening,' said Larry. 'Fatty tells us he saw a tramp. Well, we must find that tramp and somehow try to discover if he had anything to do with the fire. There's Mrs Minns, the cook, too. We must find out about her.'

'Oughtn't we to find out if anyone had a spite against Mr Hick?' put in Daisy. 'People don't go burning down cottages just for fun. It must have been done to pay Mr Hick out for something, don't you think?'

'That's a very good point, Daisy,' said Larry. 'That's one of the things we will have to discover – who had a spite against Mr Hick.'

'I should think about a hundred people had,' said Pip. 'Our gardener said that he's got a very bad temper and nobody likes him.'

'Well, if we could find out if anyone with a spite was in the garden yesterday evening, we've as good as got the man!' said Larry.

'Also we must find clues,' put in Fatty, who could not be quiet any longer.

'Glues,' said Bets joyfully. She loved the sound of that word. 'What *are* glues?'

'Bets, you really are a baby,' said Pip. 'It's not glues, it's clues.'

'Well, what are clues?' asked Bets.

'Clues are things that help us to find out what we want to know,' said Larry. 'For instance, in a detective story I was reading the other day, a thief dropped a cigarette end in the shop he was burgling, and when the police picked it up, they found it was an unusual kind of cigarette. They went round trying to find out who smoked that kind, and when at last they found out, they had got the thief! So the cigarette end was a clue.'

'I see,' said Bets. 'I shall find heaps of glues – I mean clues. I shall love that.'

'We must all keep our eyes and ears open for clues of any sort,' said Larry. 'Now, for instance, we might find footprint clues. You know – footprints leading to the cottage, made by the criminal.'

Fatty laughed scornfully. The others looked at him. 'What's the joke?' asked Larry coldly.

'Oh, nothing,' said Fatty. 'It just made me laugh a bit when I thought of you hunting for footprints in Mr Hick's garden. There can't be less than about a million, I should think – with all the people who were there watching the fire last night.'

Larry went red. He glared at Fatty's round face, and Fatty grinned back.

'The man who started the fire might have been hiding in the hedge or somewhere, waiting for his chance,' said Larry. 'Nobody went into the hedge last night. We might find footprints there, mightn't we? In the ditch, where it's muddy?'

'Yes, we might,' said Fatty. 'But it's no good looking for footprints leading to the cottage! Mine are there, and yours, and old Clear-Orf's, and a hundred others.'

'I vote we don't let Clear-Orf know we are solving the mystery,' said Pip.

'It's *his* mystery!' said Daisy. 'He's as pleased as a dog with two tails because he's got a real crime to solve.'

'Well, we'll keep out of Clear-Orf's way,' said Larry. 'Won't he look silly when we tell him who really did do it! Because I'm sure we shall find out, you know, if we all work together and try hard.'

'What shall we do for a beginning?' asked Pip, who was longing to do something.

'We must look for clues. We must find out more

about the tramp in the torn mackintosh and old hat that Fatty saw,' said Larry. 'We must find out if anyone has a spite against Mr Hick. We must find out if anyone had the chance of getting into the workroom that day, to set fire to it.'

'It wouldn't be a bad idea to talk to Mrs Minns, the cook,' said Daisy. 'She would know if anyone had been about that day. And hasn't Mr Hick got another man-servant besides his chauffeur?'

'Yes, he's got a valet, but I don't know his name,' said Larry. 'We'll find out about him too. Golly, we've got a lot to do.'

'Let's all go and look for glues first,' said Bets, who quite thought she would find all kinds of things round and about the burnt cottage, which would tell at once who the wrong-doer might be.

'Right,' said Larry, who rather wanted to hunt for clues himself. 'Now, listen – we may be turned off if any one sees us poking about at the bottom of Mr Hick's garden. So I shall drop a coin some-where, and if we are questioned I shall say I've dropped a coin, and then they'll think we are looking for it. It'll be quite true – I *shall* drop a coin!'

'All right,' said Pip, getting up. 'Come on. Let's go now – and after that I should think the next thing to do is for one of us to go and have a talk with Mrs Minns. I bet she'll be glad enough to jabber about everything. We might learn a lot of useful things from her.'

Buster leapt down from Larry's knee, his tail wagging. 'I believe he understood every word!' said Bets. 'He's just as keen to look for glues as we are!'

'You and your glues!' said Larry, laughing. 'Come on, Find-Outers! This is going to be exciting!'

4. CLUES – AND CLEAR-ORF!

The five children and Buster made their way down the drive and into the lane. They passed Mr Hick's house, and went on down the winding lane until they came to where the cottage had been burnt down. There was a tiny wooden gate that opened on to an overgrown path leading to the cottage. The children planned to go down that, because then, they hoped, nobody would see them.

There was a horrid smell of smoke and burning still on the air. It was a still April day, very sunny and warm. Celandines lay in golden sheets everywhere.

The children opened the wooden gate and went up the overgrown path. There stood what was left of the workroom, a ruined, blackened heap. It had been a very small cottage, once two-roomed, but the dividing wall had been taken down by Mr Hick, and then there had been one big room suitable for him to work in.

'Now,' said Larry, half-whispering. 'We've got to look about and see if we can find anything to help us.'

It was plainly no use to look about where all the watchers had been the night before. The garden was completely trampled down just there, and the criss-cross of footprints was everywhere. The children separated, and very solemnly began to hunt about alongside the overgrown path to the cottage, and in the tall hedges that overhung the ditches at the bottom of the garden.

Buster looked too, but as he had a firm idea that everyone was hunting for rabbits, he put his nose down each rabbit hole, and scraped violently and hopefully. It always seemed to him a great pity that rabbits didn't make their holes big enough for dogs. How easy, then, to chase a scampering bunny!

'Look at Buster hunting for clues,' said Pip, with a giggle.

The children looked for footprints. There were none on the path. They looked about in the celandines that grew in their hundreds beside the path. But there was nothing to be seen there either.

Pip wandered off to a ditch over which hung a drooping hedge of bramble and wild rose. And there he found something! He gave a low and excited call to the others.

'Here! I say, come here! I've found something!'

At once every one crowded over to him, Buster too, his nose quivering. 'What is it?' said Larry.

Pip pointed into the muddy ditch beside him. Nettles grew there, and they were trampled down. It was plain that someone had stood there in the ditch – and the only reason for standing in nettles in a muddy ditch was to hide!

'But that's not all!' said Pip, excited. 'Look – here's where the person came in and went out!'

He pointed to the hedge behind, and the children saw a gap there, with broken and bent sprays and twigs, showing where someone had forced his way in and out.

'Oooh,' said Daisy, her eyes very wide. 'Is this a clue, Larry?'

'A very big one,' said Larry, pleased. 'Pip, have you seen any footprints?'

Pip shook his head. 'The man who hid here

seemed to tread on the nettles all the time,' he said. 'Look, you can see where he went – keeping in the ditch. See where the nettles are broken down.'

The children cautiously followed the broken-down patches of nettles. The ditch curved round to the back of the cottage – but there, unfortunately, so many people had trampled the night before, that it was impossible to pick out any footsteps and say, 'Those are the man's!'

'Well, look here, although we can't find any footsteps in the garden that belong to the hiding man, we might be able to find some on the other side of the hedge,' said Fatty. 'What about us all squeezing through that gap where the man got in and out, and seeing if we can spy anything the other side.'

They all scrambled through the hole in the hedge. Fatty was the last. His eye caught sight of something as he squeezed through. It was a bit of grey flannel, caught on a thorn.

He gave a low whistle and clutched at Larry, who was just in front of him. He pointed to the scrap of flannel.

'The man tore his coat as he got through this

gap,' he said. 'See that? My word, we *are* getting on! We know that the man wore a grey flannel suit now!'

Larry carefully took off the scrap of grey rag from the thorn. He put it into a match box, wishing that he, and not Fatty, had noticed it.

'Good for you!' he said. 'Yes – that may be a very valuable clue.'

'Has Fatty found a glue?' asked Bets, in excitement. Every one crowded round to hear what Fatty had discovered. Larry opened the match box and showed the bit of grey flannel.

'Now we've only got to find some one who wears a suit of grey flannel, a bit torn somewhere, and we've got the man!' said Daisy, pleased.

'I think we're much cleverer than Clear-Orf,' said Pip.

'I've got awfully sharp eyes, you know,' said Fatty, feeling tremendously pleased with himself. 'Fancy, no one but me saw that! I really have got brains.'

'Shut up!' said Larry. 'It was just chance, that's all, that you saw it.' He put the scrap back into his match box.

Everyone felt a bit excited. 'I like being a Find-Outer,' said Bets happily.

'Well, I don't know why,' said Pip. 'You haven't found out anything yet. I found the place where the man hid, and Fatty found a bit of his coat! *You* haven't found a thing!'

It was Larry who found the footprint. He found it quite by accident. The gap in the hedge led to a grassy field, where it was impossible to see any prints at all. But the farmer had been along and taken a few squares of turf from a certain part, and at one side, near the edge, was a distinct footprint!

'It's the farmer's, I expect,' said Pip, when Larry showed it to him.

'No – there's the farmer's print,' said Larry, pointing to a big hob-nailed print, which appeared up and down the bare patch. 'This is a smaller print altogether. I shouldn't think it's more than size eight, and the farmer's footprint looks like size twelve! It's enormous. I think this *must* be the print of the man we are looking for. Let's see if we can find another.'

The children hunted about. Nothing could be seen on the grass, of course, so they went to the edges of the field. And there Daisy found three or four more footprints, some on each side of the stile that led out of the field into a lane beyond.

'Are these the same prints?' she called. The others came running. They looked hard. Larry nodded his head. 'I believe they are,' he said. 'Look – these shoes have rubber soles with criss-cross markings on them. Pip, run back to that other print, and see if the marking is the same, will you?'

Pip tore over to the patch from which the farmer had removed the turf. Yes – the criss-cross marking showed up quite clearly in the print. It was the same shoe, no doubt about that!

'Yes!' he yelled. 'It's the same!' The others were thrilled. They really were getting on!

'Well,' said Larry, looking down the lane. 'I'm afraid it's not much good going any further, because the surface of the lane is hard, and won't show anything. But we've found out what we wanted to know. We've found out that a man hid in the hedge for some reason, and we know that he wore shoes of a certain shape and size, with rubber soles that had criss-cross markings! Not bad for a day's work!'

'I'll make a drawing of the prints,' said Fatty. 'I'll

measure the exact size, and make an exact copy of the marks. Then we've only got to find the shoes, and we've got the man!'

'We know what sort of shoes he wore and what kind of suit,' said Larry, thinking of the scrap of grey cloth in his match box. 'I bet old Clear-Orf won't have noticed anything at all.'

'I'd better go back to the hotel and get some paper to copy the footprints,' said Fatty importantly. 'It's a good thing I can draw so well. I won first prize last term for art.'

'What art?' said Larry. 'The art of boasting?'

'Aren't you clever?' said Fatty crossly, who did not at all like this sort of teasing.

'Yes, he *is* clever!' said Daisy, 'but he doesn't boast about his brains as you do, Frederick Algernon Trotteville!'

'Let's go back to the burnt cottage and see if there's any other clue to be found there,' said Pip, seeing that a quarrel was about to flare up.

'Yes,' said Bets. 'I'm the only one that hasn't found a glue, and I do want to.'

She looked so sad about this that Fatty hastened to comfort her.

'Well, Buster hasn't found anything either,' he said. 'He's looked hard, but he hasn't discovered a single thing. Don't worry, Bets. I expect you will soon find something marvellous.'

They all went back to the gap in the hedge and squeezed through. Fatty went off to the little hotel opposite the garden to get a piece of paper and a pencil. The others stood and stared at the ruined cottage.

'What are you doing here?' suddenly said a rough voice. 'Clear orf!'

'Golly! It's old Clear-Orf!' whispered Larry. 'Look for my coin, all of you!'

The four children began to hunt around, pretending to be looking for something.

'Did you hear what I said?' growled the policeman. 'What are you looking for?'

'My coin,' said Larry.

'Oh! I suppose you dropped it when you came round interfering last night,' said Mr Goon. 'I don't know what children are coming to nowadays – always turning up and messing about and hindering others and being a general nuisance! You clear orf!'

'Ah! My coin!' said Larry, suddenly pouncing on his coin, which, when he had arrived, he had carefully dropped beside a patch of celandines. 'All right, Mr Goon. We'll go. I've got my coin now.'

'Well, clear orf, then,' growled the policeman. 'I've got work to do here – serious work, and I don't want children messing about, either.'

'Are you looking for glues?' asked Bets, and immediately got such a nudge from Pip that she almost fell over.

Luckily Clear-Orf took no notice of this remark. He hustled the children out of the gate and up the lane. 'And don't you come messing about here again,' he said.

'Messing about!' said Larry indignantly, as they all went off up the lane. 'That's all he thinks children do – mess about. If he knew what we'd discovered this morning, he'd go green in the face!'

'Would he really?' said Bets, interested. 'I'd like to see him.'

'You nearly made *me* go green in the face when you asked old Clear-Orf if he was looking for clues!' said Pip crossly. 'I thought the very next minute you'd say *we* had been looking for some and had found them, too! That's the worst of having a baby like you in the Find-Outers!'

'I would *not* have said we'd found anything,' said Bets, almost in tears. 'Oh, look – there's Fatty. We'd better warn him that Clear-Orf is down there.'

They stopped Fatty and warned him. He decided to go down and do his measuring and copying later on. He didn't at all like Clear-Orf. Neither did Buster.

'It's teatime, anyway,' said Larry, looking at his watch. 'Meet tomorrow morning at ten o'clock in Pip's summerhouse. We've done awfully well today. I'll write up notes about all our clues. This is really getting very exciting!'

5. FATTY AND LARRY LEARN
A FEW THINGS

At ten o'clock the next morning the five children and Buster were once again in the old summer-house. Fatty looked important. He produced an enormous sheet of paper on which he had drawn the right and left footprint, life-size, with all its criss-cross markings on the rubber sole. It was really very good.

The others stared at it. 'Not bad, is it?' said Fatty, swelling up with importance, and, as usual, making a bad impression on the others by boasting.

'Didn't I tell you I was good at drawing?'

Larry nudged Pip and whispered in his ear. 'Pull his leg a bit,' he said. Pip grinned, and wondered what Larry was going to do. Larry took the drawing and looked at it solemnly.

'Quite good, except that I think you've got the tail a bit wrong,' he said. Pip joined in at once.

'Well, I think the ears are the wrong shape too,'

he said. 'At least, the one on the right is.'

Fatty gaped, and looked at his drawing to make sure it was the right one. Yes – it was a copy of the footprints all right. Then what were Larry and Pip talking about?

'Of course, they say that hands are the most difficult things to draw,' said Larry, looking at the drawing carefully again, his head on one side. 'Now, I think Fatty ought to learn a bit more about hands.'

Daisy tried to hide a giggle. Bets was most amazed, and looked at the drawing, trying to discover the tail, ears and hands that Larry and Pip were so unaccountably chatting about. Fatty went purple with rage.

'I suppose you think you're being funny again,' he said, snatching the drawing out of Larry's hand. 'You know quite well this is a copy of the footprints.'

'Golly! So that's what it is!' said Pip, in an amazed voice. 'Of course! Larry, how could we have thought they were anything else?'

Daisy went off into a squeal of laughter. Fatty folded up the paper and looked thoroughly offended. Buster jumped up on to his knee and licked his master's nose.

Bets put everything right in her simple manner. 'Well!' she said, astonished, 'it was all a joke, wasn't it, Larry? I looked at that drawing and I could quite well see it was a really marvellous copy of those footprints we saw. I couldn't imagine what you and Pip were talking about. Fatty, I wish I could draw as well as you can!'

Fatty had got up to go, but now he sat down again. The others grinned. It was a shame to tease poor old Fatty, but really he did have such a very good opinion of himself!

'I've just shortly written down a few notes about yesterday,' said Larry, drawing a small notebook out of his pocket. He opened it and read quickly the list of clues they already had. He held out his hand for Fatty's drawing.

'I think it had better go with the notes,' he said. 'I'll keep both the notes and the drawings and the scrap of grey cloth somewhere carefully together, because they may soon become important. Where shall we keep them?'

'There's a loose board just behind you in the

wall of the summerhouse,' said Pip eagerly. 'I used to hide things there when I was little like Bets. It would be a fine place to put anything now – no one would ever think of looking there.'

He showed the others the loose board. Buster was most interested in it, stood up on the bench and scraped hard at it.

'He thinks there's a rabbit behind it,' said Bets.

The notebook, the match box with the grey rag, and Fatty's drawing were carefully put behind the loose board, which was then dragged into place again. All the children felt pleased to have a hidey-hole like that.

'Now what are our plans for today?' said Pip. 'We must get on with the solving of the mystery, you know. We don't want the police to find out everything before we do!'

'Well, one or more of us must interview Mrs Minns, the cook,' said Larry. He saw that Bets did not understand what interviewing was. 'That means we must go and see what the cook has to say about the matter,' he explained. Bets nodded.

'I could do that,' she said.

'You!' said Pip scornfully. 'You'd tell her right out

all that we had done and found and everything! You can't even keep the very smallest secret!'

'I don't tell secrets now,' said Bets. 'You know I don't. I haven't told a single secret since I was six years old.'

'Shut up, you two,' said Larry. 'I think Daisy and Pip might go and see Mrs Minns. Daisy is good at that sort of thing, and Pip can keep a look out to see that Clear-Orf or Mr Hick don't come along and guess what Daisy is doing.'

'What shall I do, Larry?' asked Fatty, quite humbly, for once in a way.

'You and I could go and talk to the chauffeur,' said Larry. 'He might let out something that would be useful to us. He usually washes down the car in the morning.'

'What about *me*?' said Bets, in dismay. 'Aren't I to do anything? I'm a Find-Outer too.'

'There's nothing you can do,' said Larry.

Bets looked very miserable. Fatty was sorry for her. 'We shan't want Buster with us,' he said. 'Do you think you could take him for a walk over the fields? He just loves a good rabbitty walk.'

'Oh yes, I could do that,' said Bets, brightening

up at once. 'I should like that. And, you never know, I might find a glue on the way.'

Everyone laughed. Bets simply could *not* remember the way to pronounce that word. 'Yes – you go and find a really important glue,' said Larry.

So Bets set off with Buster at her heels. She went down the lane towards the fields, and the others heard her telling Buster that he could look for rabbits and she would look for glues.

'Now then, to work!' said Larry, getting up. 'Daisy, you and Pip go down to Mrs Minns.'

'What excuse shall we give for going to see her?' asked Daisy.

'Oh, you must think of something yourself,' said Larry. 'Use your brains. That's what detectives do. Pip will think of something, if you can't.'

'Better not all go down the lane together,' said Pip. 'You and Fatty go first, and see if you can find the chauffeur at work, and Daisy and I will come a bit later.'

Larry and Fatty went off. They walked down the lane and came to Mr Hick's house, which stood a good way back, in its own drive. The garage was at the side of the house. A loud whistling came from that direction, and the sound of water.

'He's washing the car,' said Larry, in a low voice. 'Come on. We'll pretend we want to see someone who doesn't live here, and then ask if he'd like us to help him.'

The boys went down the drive together. They soon came in sight of the garage, and Larry went up to the young man who was hosing the car.

'Morning,' he said. 'Does Mrs Thompson live here?'

'No,' said the young man. 'This is Mr Hick's house.'

'Oh,' said Larry, in a vexed tone. Then he stared at the car.

'That's a fine car, isn't it?' he said.

'Yes, it's a Rolls Royce,' said the chauffeur. 'Fine to drive. She's very dirty today, though. I've got all my work cut out to get her clean before the master wants her this morning!'

'We'll help you,' said Larry eagerly. 'I'll hose her for you. I often do it for my father.'

In less than a minute the two boys were at work helping the young chauffeur, and the talk turned on to the fire.

'Funny business that fire,' said the chauffeur,

rubbing the bonnet of the car with a polishing cloth. 'The master was properly upset about losing those valuable papers of his. And now they say it was a put-up job – someone did it on purpose! Well – Peeks did say that it was a wonder no one had given Mr Hick a slap in the face for the way he treats everybody!'

'Who's Peeks?' said Larry, pricking up his ears.

'Peeks was his man-servant – sort of valet and secretary mixed,' said the chauffeur. 'He's gone now – went off the day of the fire.'

'Why did he go?' asked Fatty innocently.

'Got kicked out!' said the chauffeur. 'Mr Hick gave him his money, and he went! My word, there was a fine old quarrel between them, too!'

'Whatever about?' said Larry.

'Well, it seems that Mr Hick found out that Peeks sometimes wore his clothes,' said the chauffeur. 'You see, he and the master were much of a size, and Peeks used to fancy himself a bit – I've seen him prance out in Mr Hick's dark blue suit, and his blue tie with the red spots, and his gold-topped stick too!'

'Oh,' said Fatty. 'And I suppose when Mr Hick

found that out he was angry and told Mr Peeks to go. Was Mr Peeks very upset?'

'You bet he was!' said the chauffeur. 'He came out to me, and the things he said about the master would make anybody's ears burn. Then off he went about eleven o'clock. His old mother lives in the next village, and I guess she was surprised to see Horace Peeks marching in, baggage and all, at that time of the morning!'

The two boys were each thinking the same thing. It looks as if Mr Peeks burnt the cottage! We must find Mr Peeks and see what he was doing that evening!

There came a roar from a window overhead. 'Thomas! Is that car done yet? What are you jabbering about down there? Do I pay you for jabbering? No, I do not.'

'That's the master,' said Thomas, in a low tone. 'You'd better clear out. Thanks for your help.'

The boys looked up at the window. Mr Hick stood there, a cup of tea or cocoa in his hand, looking down furiously.

'Mr Hick and cup,' said Larry, with a giggle. 'Dear old good-tempered Hiccup!'

Fatty exploded into a laugh. 'We'll call him Hiccup,' he said. 'I say – we've got some news this morning, haven't we! I bet it was Mr Peeks, Larry. I bet it was!'

'I wonder how Daisy and Pip are getting on,' said Larry, as they went down the drive. 'I believe I can hear them chattering away somewhere. I guess they won't have such exciting news as we have!'

6. MRS MINNS DOES A LOT OF TALKING

Daisy and Pip were getting on very well indeed. As they had stood outside Mr Hick's garden, debating what excuse they could make for going to the kitchen door, they had heard a little mew.

Daisy looked to see where the sound came from. 'Did you hear that?' she asked Pip. The mew came again. Both children looked up into a tree, and there, unable to get down or up, was a small black and white kitten.

'It's got stuck,' said Daisy. 'Pip, can you climb up and get it?'

Pip could and did. Soon he was handing down the little creature to Daisy, and she cuddled it against her.

'Where does it belong?' she wondered.

'Probably to Mrs Minns, the cook,' said Pip promptly. 'Anyway, it will make a marvellous excuse for going to the kitchen door, and asking!'

49

'Yes, it will,' said Daisy, pleased. So the two of them set off down the drive, and went to the kitchen entrance, which was on the opposite side of the house to the garage.

A girl of about sixteen was sweeping the yard, and from the kitchen nearby there came a never-ending voice.

'And don't you leave any bits of paper flying around my yard, either, Lily! Last time you swept that yard you left a broken bottle there, and half a newspaper and goodness knows what else! Why your mother didn't teach you how to sweep and dust and bake, I *don't* know! Women nowadays just leave their daughters to be taught by such as me, that's got all their work cut out looking after a particular gentleman like Mr Hick, without having to keep an eye on a lazy girl like you!'

This was all said without a single pause. The girl did not seem to be paying any attention at all, but went on sweeping slowly round the yard, the dust flying before her.

'Hello,' said Pip. 'Does this kitten belong here?'

'Mrs Minns!' shouted the girl. 'Here's some children with the kitten.'

Mrs Minns appeared at the door. She was a round, tubby woman, short and panting, with sleeves rolled up above her elbows.

'Is this your kitten?' asked Pip again, and Daisy held it out to show the cook.

'Now where did it get to this time?' said Mrs Minns, taking it, and squeezing it against her. 'Sweetie! Sweetie! Here's your kitten again! Why don't you look after it better?'

A large black and white cat strolled out of the kitchen, and looked inquiringly at the kitten. The kitchen mewed and tried to jump down.

'Take your kitten, Sweetie,' said Mrs Minns. She put it down and it ran to its mother.

'Isn't it exactly like its mother?' said Daisy.

'She's got two more,' said Mrs Minns. 'You come in and see them. Dear little sweets! Dogs I can't bear, but give me a cat and kittens and I'm happy.'

The two children went into the kitchen. The big black and white cat had got into a basket, and the children saw three black and white kittens there too, all exactly alike.

'Oh, can I stay and play with them a bit?' asked

51

Daisy, thinking it would be a marvellous excuse to stop and talk to Mrs Minns.

'So long as you don't get into my way,' said Mrs Minns, dumping down a tin of flour on the table. She was going to make pastry. 'Where do you live?'

'Not far away, just up the lane,' answered Pip. 'We saw the fire the other night.'

That set Mrs Minns off at once. She put her hands on her hips and nodded her head till her cheeks shook.

'What a shock that was!' she said. 'My word, when I saw what was happening, anyone could have knocked me down with a feather.'

Both the children felt certain that nothing short of a bar of iron would ever knock Mrs Minns over. Daisy stroked the kittens whilst the cook went on with her talk, quite forgetting about the pastry.

'I was sitting here in my kitchen, treating myself to a cup of cocoa, and telling my sister this, that and the other,' she said. 'I was tired with turning out the store-cupboards that day, and glad enough to sit and rest my bones. And suddenly my sister says to me, "Maria!" she says, "I smell burning!" '

The children stared at her. Mrs Minns was

pleased to have such an interested audience.

'I said to Hannah – that's my sister – I said "Something burning! That's not the soup catching in the saucepan surely?" And Hannah says, "Maria, there's something burning terrible!" And then I looked out of the window and I saw something flaring up at the bottom of the garden!'

'What a shock for you!' said Daisy.

'Well!' I says to my sister, 'it looks as if the master's workroom is on fire! Glory be!' I says. 'What a day this has been! First Mr Peeks gets the sack and walks out, baggage and all. Then Mr Smellie comes along and he and the master go for one another, hammer and tongs! Then that dirty old tramp comes and the master catches him stealing eggs from the hen-house! And now if we haven't got a fire!'

The two children listened intently. All this was news to them. Goodness! There seemed to have been quite a lot of quarrels and upsets on the day of the fire. Pip asked who Mr Peeks was.

'He was the master's man-servant and secretary,' said Mrs Minns. 'Stuck-up piece of goods he was. I never had much time for him myself. Good thing he went, *I* say. *And* I shouldn't be surprised if he had something to do with that fire, either!'

But here Lily had something to say. 'Mr Peeks was *far* too much of a gentleman to do a thing like that,' she said, clattering her broom into a corner. 'If you ask me, it's old Mr Smellie.'

The children could hardly believe that anyone could be called by such a name. 'Is that his *real* name?' asked Pip.

'It surely is,' said Mrs Minns, 'and a dirty neglected old fellow he is too! What his house-keeper can be about, I don't know. She doesn't mend him up at all – sends him out with holes in his socks, and tears in his clothes, and his hat wanting brushing. He's a learned old gentleman, too, so they say, and knows more about old books and things than almost any one in the country.'

'Why did he and Mr Hick quarrel?' asked Pip.

'Goodness knows!' said Mrs Minns. 'Always quarrelling, they are. They both know a lot, but they don't agree about what they know. Anyway, old Mr Smellie, he walks out of the house muttering and grumbling, and bangs the door behind him so hard that my saucepans almost jump off the stove! But as for him setting fire to the cottage, as Lily says, don't you believe a word of it! It's my belief he wouldn't know how to set light to a bonfire! It's that stuck-up Mr Peeks who'd be spiteful enough to pay Mr Hick back, you mark my words!'

'He would not,' said Lily, who seemed determined to stick up for the valet. 'He's a nice young man, he is. You've no right to say things like that, Mrs Minns.'

'Now, look here, my girl!' said the cook, getting angry, 'if you think you can talk like that to me, you're mistaken! Telling me I've no right to say this, that and the other! You just wait till you can scrub a floor properly, and dust the tops of the pictures, and see a cobweb when it's staring you in the face, before you begin to talk big to me!'

'I wasn't talking big,' said poor Lily. 'All I said was . . .'

'Now don't you start all over again!' said Mrs Minns, thumping on the table with the rolling-pin as if she was hitting poor Lily on the head with it. 'You go and get me the butter, if you can find out where you put it yesterday. And no more backchat from *you*, if you please!'

The children didn't want to hear about Lily's faults, or where she put the butter. They wanted to hear about the people that Mr Hick had quarrelled with, and who might therefore have a spite against him. It looked as if both Mr Peeks and Mr Smellie would have spites against him. And what about the old tramp too?

'Was Mr Hick very angry with the tramp when he found him stealing the eggs?' asked Pip.

'Angry! You could hear him all over the house and the garden too!' said Mrs Minns, thoroughly enjoying talking about everything. 'I said to myself, "Ah, there's the master off again! It's a pity he doesn't use up some of his temper on that lazy girl Lily!" '

Lily appeared, looking sulky. The children couldn't help feeling sorry for her. The girl put the butter down on the table with a bang.

'Any need to try and break the basin?' inquired Mrs Minns. 'It's a bad girl you are today, a right down bad girl. You go and wash the back steps, madam! That will keep you busy for a bit.'

Lily went out, clanking a pail. 'Tell us about the tramp,' said Pip. 'What time did Mr Hick see him stealing eggs?'

'Oh, sometime in the morning,' said Mrs Minns, rolling out pastry with a heavy hand. 'The old fellow came to my back door first, whining for bread and meat, and I sent him off. I suppose he slipped round the garden to the hen-house, and the master saw him there from the cottage window. My word, he went for him all right, and said he'd call the police in, and the old tramp, he went flying by my kitchen door as if a hundred dogs were after him!'

'Perhaps *he* set fire to the cottage,' said Pip. But Mrs Minns would not have it that any one had set fire to the cottage but Mr Peeks.

'He was a sly one,' she said. 'He'd come down at nights, when everyone was in bed, and he'd go into my kitchen and take out a meat pie or a few buns or anything he'd a mind to. Well, what I say is, if someone can do that, they'll set fire to a cottage too.'

Pip remembered with a very guilty feeling that once, being terribly hungry, he had slipped down to the school kitchen and eaten some biscuits. He wondered if he was also capable of setting fire to a cottage, but he felt sure he could never do that. He didn't think that Mrs Minns was right there.

Suddenly, from somewhere in the house, there came the sound of a furious flow of words. Mrs Minns cocked her head up, listened and nodded.

'That's the master,' she said. 'Fallen over something, I shouldn't wonder.'

Sweetie, the big black and white cat, suddenly flew into the kitchen, her fur up, and her tail in the air. Mrs Minns gave a cry of woe.

'Oh, Sweetie! Did you get under his feet again! Poor lamb, poor darling lamb!'

The poor darling lamb retired under the table, hissing. The three kittens in the basket stiffened in alarm, and hissed too. Mr Hick appeared in the kitchen, looking extremely angry.

'Mrs Minns! I have once more fallen over that horrible cat of yours. How many more times am I to tell you to keep her under control? Why you want to keep such an ugly and vicious animal, I cannot think,' he said. 'And good heavens above – are those kittens in that basket?'

'They are, sir, said Mrs Minns, her voice rising high. 'And good homes I've found for every single one of them, when they're old enough.'

Mr Hick then saw the two children, and appeared to be just as displeased to see them as he had been to see the kittens.

'What are these children doing here?' he asked sharply. 'You ought to know better, Mrs Minns, than to keep your kitchen full of tiresome children and wretched cats and kittens! Tell them to go!'

He marched out of the door, first setting down the empty cup and saucer he was carrying. Mrs Minns glared after him.

'For two pins I'd burn your precious cottage down if it wasn't already gone!' she called after Mr Hick, when he was safely out of hearing. Sweetie rubbed against her skirt, purring loudly. She bent down and stroked her.

'Did the nasty man tramp on you?' she asked fondly. 'Did he say nasty things about the dear little kittens? Never you mind, Sweetie!'

'We'd better be going,' said Daisy, afraid that Mr Hick might hear what Mrs Minns was saying, and come back in a worse temper than ever. 'Thank you for all you've told us, Mrs Minns. It was most interesting.'

Mrs Minns was pleased. She presented Pip and Daisy with a ginger bun each. They thanked her and went, bubbling over with excitement.

'We've learnt such a lot that it's going to be difficult to sort it all out!' said Pip. 'It seems as if at least three people might have done the crime – and really, if that's the kind of way that Mr Hick usually behaves I can't help feeling there must be about twenty people who would only be too glad to pay him back for something!'

7. THE TRAMP – CLEAR-ORF – AND FATTY!

The four children met in the old summerhouse all full of excitement. Bets and Buster were not yet back, but they couldn't wait for them to come. They had to tell their news.

'We saw the chauffeur! He's called Thomas,' said Larry. 'He told us all about the valet called Mr Peeks. He was chucked out on the day of the fire, for wearing his master's clothes!'

'I'm sure he did the crime,' said Fatty eagerly. 'We must find out more about him. He lives in the next village.'

'Yes, but listen!' said Daisy. 'It might be old Mr Smellie!'

'*Who*?' said Larry and Fatty, in astonishment. 'Mr *Smellie*!'

'Yes,' said Daisy, with a giggle. '*We* thought it couldn't be a real name, too, when we heard it, but it is.'

'Mr Hiccup and Mr Smellie,' said Fatty unexpectedly. 'What a lovely pair!'

Larry chuckled. 'Daisy and Pip don't know about Mr Hick and cup,' he said. He told them. They laughed.

'It isn't *really* very funny, but it *seems* as if it is,' said Daisy. 'At school things seem like that sometimes too – we scream with laughter, and afterwards it doesn't really seem funny at all. But do let us tell you about Mr Smellie, and the quarrel he had with Mr Hiccup.'

She told Larry and Fatty all that Mrs Minns had said. Then Pip told about the old tramp who had been caught stealing eggs. And then Daisy described how Mr Hick himself had come into the kitchen and rowed Mrs Minns for letting her cat get under his feet. 'They had a proper quarrel,' said Daisy, 'and Mrs Minns actually called after Mr Hick and said she felt like burning down his cottage if it hadn't already been done!'

'Golly!' said Larry, surprised. 'It looks as if old Mrs Minns might have done it herself then – if she felt like it today, she might quite easily have felt like it two days ago – and done it! She had plenty of chance.'

'You know, we have already found four suspects,' said Fatty solemnly. 'I mean – we can quite properly suspect four persons of setting fire to that cottage – the old tramp, Mr Smellie, Mr Peeks and Mrs Minns! We *are* getting on.'

'Getting on?' said Larry. 'Well, I don't know about that. We seem to find more and more people to suspect, which makes it all more and more difficult. I can't think how in the world we're going to discover which it is.'

'We must find out the movements of the four suspects,' said Fatty wisely. 'For instance, if we find out that Mr Smellie, whoever he is, spent the evening of the day before yesterday fifty miles away from here, we can rule him out. And if we find that Horace Peeks was at home with his mother all that evening, we can rule *him* out. And so on.'

'What we shall probably find is that all four people were messing about somewhere near the place,' said Pip. 'And how in the world are we going to trace that old tramp? You know what tramps are – they wander about for miles, and nobody knows where they go or where they come from.'

'Yes – the tramp's going to be difficult,' said Daisy. 'Very difficult. We can't rush all over the country looking for a tramp. And if we did find him, it's going to be difficult to ask him if he set fire to the cottage.'

'We needn't do that, silly,' said Larry. 'Have you forgotten our clues?'

'What do you mean?' asked Daisy.

'Well – we've only got to find out what size shoes he wears, and if they've got rubber soles, criss-crossed with markings underneath, and if he wears a grey flannel coat,' said Larry.

'He doesn't wear a grey flannel coat,' said Fatty. 'I told you – he wore an old mackintosh.'

The others were silent for a moment. 'Well, he might have a grey flannel coat underneath,' said Daisy. 'He might have taken his mackintosh off for a moment.'

The others thought this was rather feeble, but they had no better suggestion.

'Time enough to worry about grey flannel coats and mackintoshes when we've found the tramp,' said Pip. 'That *is* going to be a problem, I must say!'

'Hark – isn't that old Buster barking?' said Fatty

suddenly. 'I bet that's Bets coming back. Yes – she's calling to Buster. I say – haven't we got a lot of news for her?'

The sound of Bets' running feet was heard up the drive, and then down the garden path to the summerhouse. The four big ones went to the door to welcome her. Buster shot up to them, barking madly.

'Bets! We've got such a lot of news!' called Larry.

'We've had a most exciting time!' cried Daisy.

But Bets didn't listen. Her eyes were shining brightly, her cheeks were red with running, and she could hardly get her words out, she was so excited.

'Pip! Larry! I've got a glue! Oh, I've got a glue!'

'What?' asked the other four together.

'I've found the tramp!' panted the little girl. 'Do say he's the biggest glue we've found!'

'Well – he's really a suspect, not a clue,' began Larry, but the others interrupted him.

'Bets! Are you sure you've found the tramp?' asked Pip excitedly. 'Golly – we thought that would be almost impossible.'

'Where is he?' demanded Fatty, ready to go after him immediately.

'How do you know it's the tramp?' cried Daisy.

'Well, he was wearing a dirty old mackintosh and a terrible old hat with a hole in the crown,' said Bets. 'Just like Fatty said.'

'Yes – the hat did have a hole in the crown,' said Fatty. 'Bets, where is this fellow?'

'Well, I went for a walk with Buster, as you know,' said Bets, sinking down on the grass, tired out with running. 'He's a lovely dog to take for a walk, because he's so interested in everything. Well, we went down the lane and into the fields, and along by the river, ever so far. We came to a field where sheep and lambs were, and there was a hayrick nearby.'

Buster barked a little, as if he wanted to tell about it all too. Bets put her arm round him. 'It was Buster who found the tramp – wasn't it, darling? You see, I was walking along – and suddenly Buster went all stiff – and the hairs rose up along the back of his neck – and he growled.'

'Ur-r-r-r-rrr!' said Buster obligingly.

'He honestly understands every word, doesn't

he?' said Bets. 'Well, Buster went all funny, like that, and then he began to walk stiffly towards the hayrick – you know, just as if he had bad rheumatism or something.'

'Animals always walk like that when they are suspicious, or frightened or angry,' said Fatty, grinning at Bets. 'Go on. Don't be so long-winded.'

'I went with Buster,' said Bets, 'as quietly as I could, thinking there might be a cat or something the other side of the rick. But it was the tramp!'

'Golly!' said Larry, and Pip whistled.

'You're a very good Find-Outer,' said Fatty warmly.

'I did so badly want to find out something,' said Bets. 'But I suppose really and truly it was Buster who did the finding, wasn't it?'

'Well, he wouldn't have, if you hadn't taken him for a walk,' said Larry. 'What was the tramp doing?'

'He was asleep,' said Bets. 'Fast asleep. He didn't even wake when Buster sniffed at his feet.'

'His *feet*!' said Pip. 'What sort of shoes did he have on? Did they have rubber soles?'

Bets looked dismayed. 'Oh! I never thought of looking. And I so easily could have seen, couldn't I, because he was fast asleep. But I was so excited at finding him that I just never thought of looking at his shoes.'

'There's no time to be lost,' said Pip, jumping up. 'He may still be fast asleep. We'd better go and have a look at him and his shoes and his clothes. Fatty can tell us at once if he's the tramp he saw in Mr Hick's garden or not.'

Excited and rather solemn, the Five Find-Outers and Dog set off down the lane to the fields that ran beside the river. They went fast, in case the tramp had woken up and gone on his way. It was so marvellous that Bets should actually have found him – they couldn't possibly risk losing him!

They came to the rick. A gentle sound of snoring told them that the tramp was still there. Fatty picked up Buster and crept round the rick without making a sound.

On the other side, curled up well, lay a tramp. He was an old fellow, with a stubbly grey beard, shaggy grey eyebrows, a red nose, and long, untidy hair that straggled from under a terrible old hat. Fatty took a look at him. He tiptoed back to the others.

'Yes – it's the tramp all right!' he whispered,

thrilled. 'But it's going to be difficult to pull aside his mackintosh to see if he's got a grey coat underneath. And he's got his feet sort of curled up underneath him. We shall have to get right down on the ground to see what sort of sole his shoes have got underneath.'

'I'll go and try,' said Larry. 'You others keep Buster quiet here, and watch out in case anyone comes.'

Leaving the others on the far side of the rick, Larry crept round to the side where the tramp slept. He sat down near him. He put out his hand to pull aside the old mackintosh to see if the man wore grey underneath. The trousers appearing below the coat were so old and dirty that it was quite impossible to tell what colour they had once been.

The tramp moved a little and Larry took back his hand. He decided to try and see the underneath of the man's shoes. So he knelt down, put his head to the ground and did his best to squint at the tramp's shoes.

The tramp suddenly opened his eyes. He stared in the greatest astonishment at Larry.

'What's bitten *you*?' he suddenly said, and Larry almost jumped out of his skin.

'Think I'm the king of England, I suppose, kneeling in front of me with your head on the ground like that!' said the tramp. 'Get away. I can't abide children. Nasty interfering little creatures!'

He curled himself up again and shut his eyes. Larry waited for a second or two, and was about to try squinting at the man's shoes again when he heard a low whistle from the other side of the rick. That meant someone was coming. Well, they would all have to wait till the passer-by was gone. Larry crept round to join Pip and the rest.

'Someone coming?' he asked.

'Yes – old Clear-Orf!' said Fatty. Larry peeped round the rick. The village policeman was coming up from the other direction, along a path that did not go near the rick. He would soon be gone.

But as he came along he suddenly caught sight of the old tramp sleeping by the rick. The children drew back hurriedly as Mr Goon walked quietly and quickly over to the rick. There was a ladder leaning against the rick and Larry pushed Bets and the others up as quickly as he could. They would be less likely to be seen on top than below. Fortunately the rick had been cut well out, when hay was taken to the various farm animals, and it was easy to balance on the cut-out part.

The policeman crept up quietly. The children, peering over the rick, saw him take out a notebook. Fatty gave Larry such a nudge that the boy nearly fell.

'Look! Look what he's got down in his notebook! He's got a drawing of that footprint *we* saw! He's been cleverer than we thought!'

Clear-Orf tiptoed up to the tramp and tried his best to see what sort of shoes he had on. He, too, did as Larry had done and knelt down, the better to see. And the tramp opened his eyes!

His astonishment at seeing the policeman kneeling in front of him was enormous. It was one thing to see a boy behaving like that, but quite another thing to see a policeman. The tramp leapt to his feet with a howl.

'First it's a boy bowing down to me and now it's a bobby!' he said, jamming his old hat down on his long grey hair. 'What's it all about?'

'I want to see your shoes,' said Clear-Orf.

'Well, see them, then! Look at them well, laces and all!' said the tramp, rapidly losing his temper.

'I want to see the soles,' said the policeman stolidly.

'Are you a cobbler or a policeman?' asked the tramp. 'Well – you show me the buttons on your shirt, and I'll show you the soles of my shoes!'

The policeman began to breathe very heavily, and his face got red. He snapped his notebook shut.

'You better come-alonga me,' he said. The tramp didn't think so. He skipped out of the way and began to run across the field, very nimbly indeed for an old fellow. Clear-Orf gave a roar, and turned to run after him.

And at that moment Fatty, excited beyond words, fell off the hayrick, and landed with a thud on the ground below. He gave such an agonised yell that the policeman stopped in amazement.

'What's all this 'ere?' he said, and glared at Fatty. Then he caught sight of the other children peering anxiously down from the top of the rick, afraid that Fatty had broken all his bones. He was most astonished.

'You come on down!' he roared. 'Always

children messing about! You wait till the farmer catches you! How long have you been there? What do you mean, spying like this?'

Fatty gave a frightful groan, and the policeman, torn between his desire to rush after the disappearing tramp, and to pull Fatty to his feet, went up to him.

'Don't touch me! I think I've broken my left leg and my right arm, dislocated both my shoulders and broken my appendix!' said Fatty, who sincerely believed that he was practically killed.

Bets gave a squeal of horror and jumped down to see what she could do to help poor Fatty. The others leapt down too, and Buster danced delightedly round Clear-Orf's ankles.

'Clear orf,' he said. 'Dogs and children! Always messing about and getting in the way. Now that fellow's gone, and I've missed a chance of questioning him!'

He waited to see if Fatty was really hurt. But, except for a few bruises, Fatty was not hurt at all. He had not broken any bones!

As soon as the policeman saw the others helping Fatty up, brushing him down, and comforting him, he took a look round to see if he could make out where the tramp had gone. But he was nowhere to be seen. He turned to the five children.

'Now, clear orf,' he said. 'And don't let me see you hanging round again.'

Then, with great dignity, Mr Goon made his way heavily to the path, and walked down it without turning his head once. The children looked at each other.

'We were getting on so well till Clear-Orf came,' sighed Daisy. 'I wonder where that tramp went to.'

'I'm going home,' said Fatty miserably. 'I feel awful.'

'I'll take you home,' said Daisy. 'You come too, Bets. Do you boys want to see if you can trace the tramp?'

'Yes,' said Larry. 'Might as well whilst we've got the chance. I don't wonder Fatty fell off the rick. It was pretty exciting, wasn't it?'

'Fancy old Clear-Orf having a drawing of that footprint in his notebook,' said Pip thoughtfully. 'He's smarter than I thought. Still – we've got something he hasn't got – a bit of grey flannel!'

Fatty, Daisy, Bets and Buster went off together.

The other two set off in the direction the tramp had taken. They meant to find him again if they could!

8. WHAT MUST BE DONE NEXT?

Larry and Pip ran quickly in the direction the tramp had gone. It seemed silly that, although all the children had seen him, and Clear-Orf too, nobody had managed to find out what kind of soles his shoes had!

There was no sign of the tramp at all. The boys met a farm labourer and hailed him.

'Excuse me, have you seen an old tramp going this way?'

'Yes. Into that wood,' said the man, and pointed to a small copse of trees in the distance. The boys ran there, and looked about among the trees and tangled undergrowth.

They smelt the smoke of a fire, and their noses and eyes soon guided them to it. By it, on a fallen tree, sat the dirty old tramp, his hat off now, showing his tangled, straggly hair. He was cooking something in a tin over the fire.

When he saw Larry he scowled. 'What! You here again?' he said. 'You get away. What do you mean, following me about like this? I haven't done nothing.'

'Well,' said Larry boldly, 'you tried to steal eggs from Mr Hick's hen-house the other day. We know that! But that's nothing to do with us.'

'Mr Hick! So that's his name,' said the old tramp, sticking a skewer in whatever it was that he was cooking. 'I didn't steal his eggs! I didn't steal nothing at all. I'm an honest old fellow, I am, and everybody will tell you the same!'

'Well – what were you doing hiding in the ditch at the bottom of his garden?' said Larry. The tramp looked astonished.

'I never hid in no ditch,' he said. 'I wasn't the one that did the hiding. Ho, dear me no! I could tell you something, I could – but I'm not going to. You put that policeman after me, didn't you?'

'No,' said Larry. 'He came along unexpectedly and went over to you. He didn't know we were anywhere about.'

'Well, I don't believe you,' said the old tramp. 'You set that bobby after me. I know you did. I'm not going to be mixed up in anything that don't concern me. But there was funny goings-on that night, ho yes, I should think there were.'

The old fellow suddenly groaned and rubbed his right foot. His big toe stuck out of the shoe, which was too small for him. He took the shoe off, showing a sock that was practically all holes, and rubbed his foot tenderly.

The boys looked at the shoe, which the tramp had thrown carelessly to one side. The sole was plainly to be seen. It was of leather, and so much worn that it could not possibly keep any damp out.

'No rubber sole!' whispered Larry to Pip. 'So it couldn't have been the tramp hiding in the ditch. Anyway, I don't believe he knows a thing. And look at the old coat he's got under the mack – it's green with age, not grey!'

'What you whispering about?' said the tramp. 'You get away. Can't I live in peace? I don't do no harm to nobody, I don't, but children and bobbies, they come after me like flies. You leave me alone. I'd be as merry as a blackbird if I had a pair of shoes that fitted me poor old feet. You got a pair of shoes that would fit me?'

'What size do you take?' asked Pip, thinking that perhaps he could get an old pair of his father's boots for the footsore old tramp. But the tramp didn't know. He had never bought a pair of shoes in his life.

'Well, if I can get an old pair of my father's boots, I'll bring them to you,' said Pip. 'Or better still, you come and get them. I live in the red house in the lane not far from Mr Hick's house. You come there tomorrow, and I'll perhaps have got some boots for you.'

'You'll set that bobby after me again if I come back,' grumbled the tramp, taking out something peculiar from the tin, and beginning to eat it with his hands. 'Or that Mr Hick will. Well, he'd better be careful. I know a few things about Mr Hick and his household, I do. Yes, I heard him shouting at quite a few people that day, besides me. Ho yes. There was funny goings on there, but I'm not mixed up in them, I tell you.'

Larry looked at his watch. It was getting late. 'We'll have to go,' he said. 'But you come along to Pip's house tomorrow, and you can tell us anything you want to. We shan't give you away.'

The boys left the old tramp and tore home to

their dinner, very late indeed. Their mothers were not pleased with them.

'Whatever have you been doing?' asked Pip's mother. 'Where have you been?'

Pip couldn't possibly tell her, because the Find-Outers and their doings were very secret. 'I was with the others,' he said at last.

'You weren't, Pip,' said his mother. 'Bets and Daisy have been here a long time – and that boy too, whatever his name is. Don't tell stories.'

'Well, I was with Larry,' said Pip. Bets saw that he was in difficulties and she tried to rescue him by suddenly changing the subject.

'Fatty fell off a hayrick this morning,' she said. It certainly changed the subject. Her mother stared at her in horror.

'Who did? That boy? Did he hurt himself? Whatever were you doing on a hayrick?'

Pip was afraid that Bets was going to say why they were all on the rick, so *he* changed the subject quickly too.

'Mummy, has Daddy got a very old pair of boots he doesn't want?' he asked innocently. His mother looked at him.

'Why?' she asked. Pip was not usually interested in his father's old clothes.

'Well, I happen to know someone who would be very glad of them indeed,' said Pip.

'Why?' asked his mother again.

'Well, you see, his toes are sticking right out of his shoes,' explained Pip, trying to interest his mother in the matter.

'Whose toes?' asked his mother, astonished.

Pip stopped. Now he would have to bring in the tramp, and that was part of the secret. Bother! Whatever they talked about seemed to lead back to something the Find-Outers were doing.

'It's just a poor old tramp,' said Bets. Pip glared at her.

'A tramp!' said her mother. 'Surely you are not making friends with people like that, Pip?'

'No,' said Pip desperately. 'I'm not. I'm only sorry for him, that's all. You always say, Mummy, that we should be sorry for people not so well off as ourselves, and help them, don't you? Well, that's why I thought of giving him some old boots, that's all.'

'I see,' said his mother, and Pip gave a sigh of

relief. 'Well, I'll find out if there is an old pair of Daddy's boots, and if there is, you shall have them. Now, do get on with your dinner.'

After he had finished his very late meal, Pip escaped into the garden and went to find Bets, who was in the summerhouse.

'Bets! Was Fatty all right? He wasn't really hurt, was he?'

'No,' said Bets. 'Didn't he make a thump when he fell? Did you and Larry find the tramp? What happened?'

'Well, he's not the person who hid in the ditch, nor the one whose coat got caught on the brambles,' said Pip. 'We saw both his shoes and his coat. He heard all the quarrels that went on. Larry and I thought we'd ask him a few questions to-morrow when he comes to get the boots. I believe he could tell us quite a few things if he was certain we wouldn't put the police after him. He may even have spotted who was hiding in the ditch!'

'Oooh,' said Bets, thrilled. 'Oh, Pip, wasn't it funny when the tramp woke and saw Larry kneeling in front of him – and after that, old Clear-Orf doing the same thing!'

'Yes, it was funny,' said Pip, grinning. 'Hello, there's Fatty and Buster.'

Fatty limped into the garden, walking extremely stiffly. He had tried to make up his mind whether to act very heroically, and pooh-pooh his fall, but limp to make the others sorry for him, or whether to make out that he had hurt himself inside very badly and frighten them.

At the moment he was behaving heroically. He smiled at Bets and Pip, and sat down very gingerly.

'Do you hurt much?' asked Bets sympathetically.

'Oh, I'm all right,' said Fatty, in a very, very brave voice. 'A fall off a rick isn't much! Don't you worry about *me*!'

The others stared at him in admiration.

'Hello – here are Larry and Daisy,' said Pip.

Fatty didn't like to say anything about his bruises, though he was simply longing to show them to the others. Larry had been thinking a lot about everything whilst he had gobbled up his late dinner, and he had his plans all ready. He didn't even ask poor Fatty how he felt after his fall, but started off straightaway with his ideas.

'Look here,' he said, 'I've been thinking about

Clear-Orf. I don't like him knowing about those footprints. We don't want him to solve this mystery before we do. For all we know he's got his eye on Mr Peeks and Mr Smellie too, as well as the tramp. We *must* get in first. It would be too awful if horrid old Clear-Orf found out everything before we did!'

'It would,' agreed everyone wholeheartedly. Buster wagged his tail.

'We must see this man-servant, Mr Peeks,' said Larry. 'It's most important. I don't suspect that old tramp anymore now that I've seen his shoes and coat. Anyway, I'm certain that if he had set fire to the cottage, he would have fled away out of the district as soon as ever he could. As it is, he's still about. I don't believe he did it. I'm much more inclined to think that Mr Peeks did it. We must find out.'

'We must,' agreed every one again.

'I shall question the tramp closely tomorrow,' said Larry, rather grandly. 'I feel certain he can tell us plenty. Fatty, do you think you and Daisy could find out about Mr Peeks tomorrow? I'll stay here with Pip and Bets and question the tramp.'

'Right!' said Fatty and Daisy joyfully. If only they could get ahead of Clear-Orf! They simply must beat him!

9. LILY COMES INTO THE STORY

Fatty really didn't want to do anything more that day, so Larry, Pip and Daisy left him in the garden with Bets and Buster, reading quietly. They thought they would go down to Mr Hick's house and talk to Mrs Minns again.

'We ought really to find out if Mrs Minns could have set fire to the cottage herself,' said Larry. 'I don't feel as if she did, but you can't go by feelings if you are a detective. Also, we must get Horace Peeks's address.'

'We'll take some fish for Sweetie, the cat,' said Daisy. 'I think there was some left over that cook might let me have. Mrs Minns will be awfully pleased to see us if we take a present for Sweetie.'

The cook gave her a fish head, wrapped up in paper. Buster smelt it and wanted to follow Daisy, but Fatty held him firmly by the collar.

'It's no good him coming,' said Daisy. 'He'd be

sure to chase Sweetie, and then Mrs Minns would chase *us*!'

They went down the lane together. 'Leave me to do the talking,' said Larry.

Daisy laughed. 'Don't you worry – it will be Mrs Minns who does it!' she said.

They arrived at the kitchen door and looked inside. Lily was there, writing a letter. She looked as if she had been crying. 'Where's Mrs Minns?' asked Larry.

'Upstairs,' said Lily. 'She's in a bad temper. I upset a jug of milk all over her, and she keeps on saying I did it on purpose.'

'Were you here on the night of the fire?' asked Larry. Lily shook her head.

'Where were you, then?' asked Larry. 'Didn't you see the fire?'

'I saw it when I came back from my evening off,' said Lily. 'Never you mind where I was. It's got nothing to do with you!'

'I know,' said Larry, surprised at Lily's violent tone. 'What I can't understand is – why didn't Mrs Minns or her sister smell the fire when it began!'

'Here's Mrs Minns's sister now,' said Lily,

looking up as a very large woman, with twinkling eyes under a big hat trimmed with flowers, came up to the kitchen door. She looked in and seemed surprised to see the children.

'Hello, Mrs Jones,' said Lily sulkily. 'Mrs Minns is upstairs changing her dress. She won't be a minute.'

Mrs Jones came in and sank into a rocking-chair, breathing heavily. 'My, it's hot today,' she said. 'Who are all these children?'

'We live up the lane,' said Pip. 'We've brought a fish head for Sweetie.'

'Where are all the kittens?' asked Daisy, looking at the empty basket.

'Oh!' said Lily. 'I hope they haven't gone out of the kitchen and upstairs. Mrs Minns told me to keep the door shut!'

'Perhaps the kittens are outside,' said Larry, shutting the door that led into the hall. He didn't particularly want Mr Hick to hear the talking in the kitchen and come in. 'Oh – there's Sweetie!'

The big black and white cat came into the kitchen, her tail straight up in the air. She smelt the fish head and went to Daisy. Daisy unwrapped it and put it into the cat's dinner bowl in a corner of the kitchen. Sweetie immediately took it out of the bowl and began to eat it on the floor.

'Was Sweetie frightened of the fire the other night?' asked Pip, thinking it was about time to start on the subject.

'She was kind of restless,' said Mrs Jones.

'Oh, were *you* here?' said Daisy, pretending to be surprised. 'Goodness – how was it you didn't know the cottage was burning then?'

'I did,' said Mrs Jones indignantly. 'Didn't I keep saying to Maria, "Maria, there's something burning!" I've a very good nose, but Maria hasn't. I kept sniffing round the kitchen, and I even put my nose into the hall, thinking there might be something burning there.'

'Didn't Mrs Minns go and see if there was anything burning too?' asked Larry.

'Ah, Maria didn't want to move that evening,' said Mrs Jones. 'She'd got her rheumatism back something cruel. She was stuck, real stuck.'

'What do you mean, stuck?' asked Larry, with interest.

'Well, she sat down in this rocking-chair at

tea-time, and she says to me, "Hannah," she says, "I'm stuck. Me rheumatism's got me again, and I can't move." So I says to her, "Maria, you just stay put. I'll get the tea and everything. Mr Hick is out, so there's no dinner to get. I'll just stay with you till your poor legs are better." '

The children listened, and each of them thought the same thing. If Mrs Minns was stuck in a chair all the evening with rheumatism, then she couldn't have set fire to the cottage!

'And didn't poor Mrs Minns get up at all out of the rocking-chair?' asked Daisy. 'Not till you really knew there was a fire, I mean?'

'No – Maria just stayed put,' said Mrs Jones. 'It wasn't till me nose told me there really was something burning terrible that Maria got up. I went to the kitchen door and sniffed – and then I went out into the garden – and I saw the flare down at the bottom there. I shouted out, "There's a fire, Maria!" and she turned as white as a sheet. "Come on, Maria!" I says, "We've got to do something." But poor Maria, she can't get out of her chair, she's so stuck!'

The children drank all this in. It certainly could

have been nothing to do with Mrs Minns. If she had been so 'stuck' with rheumatism, she wouldn't have been likely to rush round setting fire to cottages. And anyway her sister was with her all the time. It was quite plainly nothing to do with Mrs Minns. That was another suspect crossed off!

Mrs Minns opened the kitchen door and came in, looking angry. She had been upstairs to take off her milk-drenched dress. She glared at Lily, and then looked in surprise at the three children.

'Well, Maria,' said Mrs Jones, 'how's the rheumatics?'

'Good afternoon, Mrs Minns,' said Daisy. 'We came to bring a fish head for Sweetie.'

Mrs Minns beamed. She was always touched when anyone did anything for her precious cat. 'That's nice of you,' she said. 'My rheumatism's better,' she said to her sister. 'Though what it will be like after being drenched with milk, I *don't* know. Really, things are coming to a pretty pass when that girl Lily throws milk all over me.'

'I didn't do it on purpose,' said Lily sulkily. 'Can I go to the post with this letter?'

'No, that you can't,' said Mrs Minns. 'You just get the tea ready for Mr Hick. Go on now – stop your letter-writing and get a bit of work done for a change.'

'I want to catch the post,' said Lily, looking ready to cry.

'Well, you won't,' said Mrs Minns unkindly. Lily started to cry, and the children felt sorry for her. She got up and began to get out cups and saucers.

The children wondered how to mention Horace Peeks. They wanted to get his address so that they might go and see him.

'Has Mr Hick got a new man-servant yet?' asked Larry, at last.

'He's been seeing some today,' said Mrs Minns, sinking into an armchair, which creaked dolefully beneath her weight. 'I only hope he gets one that doesn't put on airs and graces like Mr Peeks, that's all.'

'Does Mr Peeks live near here?' asked Pip innocently.

'Yes,' said Mrs Minns. 'Let me see now – where does he live? Oh, my memory – it gets worse every day!'

There came a most unwelcome interruption just as it seemed that Mrs Minns was on the point of remembering Horace Peeks's address. The kitchen door shot open, and three kittens flew through the air, landing on the floor with mews and hisses. Everyone looked round in amazement.

Mr Hick stood at the door, his front tuft of hair bristling like a parrot's crest.

'Those kittens were in my study!' he shouted. 'Are my orders never to be obeyed?'

He was about to bang the door when he caught sight of the three children. He advanced into the kitchen and pointed a finger at them. 'Didn't I turn you out before? How dare you come here again?'

Larry, Pip and Daisy got up and fled. They were not cowards, but really Mr Hick was so very fierce that it honestly seemed as if he might throw them out, just as he had flung the kittens into the kitchen!

They ran up the drive – but halfway to the gate Larry stopped. 'Wait till old Hiccup has gone out of the kitchen,' he said. 'We simply *must* get Horace

Peeks's address. We can't do anything about him till we know where he is.'

They waited for a minute or two and then went back very cautiously to the kitchen. Mrs Minns was talking to her sister, and Lily was still clattering about with the tea things. The children put their heads round the door.

'What do you want now?' asked Mrs Minns good-naturedly. 'My word, you ran away like frightened mice! Made me laugh to see you!'

'You were just trying to think of Horace Peeks's address when Mr Hick came in,' said Larry.

'Was I, now?' said Mrs Minns. 'Well, it came into my mind in a flash, like – and now it's gone again. Let me see – let me see . . .'

She was thinking hard, and the children were waiting breathlessly, when the sound of heavy footsteps came up to the kitchen door and a loud knock was heard.

Mrs Minns went to the door. The children saw that it was Mr Goon, the policeman! They never seemed to be able to get away from old Clear-Orf.

'Morning, madam,' said Clear-Orf to Mrs Minns,

and he took out his large black notebook. 'About this here fire – I think you've given me all the information I require. But I'd just like to ask you a few questions about that fellow Peeks.'

The children frowned at one another. So Clear-Orf was after Peeks too!

'Do you know his address?' asked Clear-Orf, looking at Mrs Minns out of his bulging pale blue eyes.

'Well,' said Mrs Minns, 'if that isn't a peculiar thing, Mr Goon – I was just trying to think of his address at the very moment you knocked! These children wanted to know it.'

'What children?' said Clear-Orf in surprise. He put his head in at the door and saw Larry, Daisy and Pip.

'You again!' he said in disgust. 'Clear orf! You kids are always popping up. You're a regular nuisance. What do you want Peeks's address for? Just nosey, I suppose?'

The children said nothing. Mr Goon pointed backwards with his thumb. 'Go home!' he said. 'I've private business to do here. Clear orf!'

There was nothing for it but to 'clear orf,' and

the children did so, running up the drive to the gate. They were very angry.

'Just as Mrs Minns was thinking of the address!' said Larry.

'I hope she doesn't think of it and tell Clear-Orf,' said Pip gloomily. 'If she does, Clear-Orf will go over and see Mr Peeks before we do.'

'Blow!' said Daisy. They all felt very disheartened. They were just going out of the gate when they heard a low whistle from the bushes nearby. They turned back to see who it was.

Lily appeared, a letter in her hand. She looked frightened, but determined. 'Will you post this letter for me?' she asked. 'It's to Mr Peeks, to warn him that people are saying he started the fire. But he didn't, he didn't. I know he didn't! You post the letter, will you?'

There was a shout from the kitchen. 'Lily! Where are you!'

Lily disappeared at once. The children ran out of the gate, excited and surprised. They stopped behind a hedge when they had gone a little way, and examined Lily's envelope. It had no stamp on. The girl had forgotten it in her hurry.

'Golly!' said Larry, 'here we've been all the afternoon trying to get Horace Peeks's address and couldn't – and now, suddenly, it's just been presented to us, given into our hands!'

'What a bit of luck!' said Daisy, thrilled. 'I *am* pleased.'

'The thing is – do we want Mr Peeks to be warned?' said Larry. 'You see – if he did do the crime, he ought to be caught and punished. There's no doubt about that. If he is warned beforehand that people are suspecting him, he might run away. Then we shouldn't solve the mystery.'

They all stared at one another. Then Pip had an idea. 'I know! We'll go and find Mr Peeks after tea today, instead of waiting for tomorrow. We'll see him and try to make up our minds if he did it or not. If we think he didn't do it, we'll give him Lily's letter!'

'Good idea!' said the others, pleased. 'After all, we can't post a letter without a stamp – but we can deliver it by hand.' They looked at the address.

> *Mr H. Peeks,*
> *Ivy Cottage,*
> *Wilmer Green*

'We'll go on our bikes,' said Larry. 'Come on – we must tell the others!'

10. INTERVIEWING MR HORACE PEEKS

The three of them went back to Fatty and Bets. Buster greeted them uproariously.

'Hello,' said Fatty, 'how did you get on?'

'Awfully badly at first,' said Larry, 'and then, right at the end, we had a slice of good luck.'

He told Bets and Fatty about the afternoon and they listened with the greatest interest. They all examined Mr Peeks's address, and were thrilled.

'So now Pip and Daisy and I are going on our bikes to Wilmer Green,' said Larry. 'It's only about five miles. At least, we'll have tea first and then go.'

'I want to go too,' said Bets at once.

'I'd *like* to go, but I don't feel up to it,' said Fatty.

'You stay with Bets,' said Pip. 'We don't want to appear in a crowd. It might put Mr Peeks on his guard.'

'You keep leaving me out,' said Bets sadly.

'No, we don't,' said Larry. 'Do you really want a

job? Well, find out Mr Smellie's address, see? Fatty will help you. It may be in the telephone book, or somebody may know it. We shall want his address tomorrow, because we must go and see him too. All the suspects must be interviewed!'

'Two of them are crossed off now,' said Pip. 'Mrs Minns didn't do it – and I'm sure the tramp didn't either. That only leaves Mr Smellie and Mr Peeks. I do wish we could find someone wearing rubber-soled shoes with those markings. It would be such a help!'

'I'll find out Mr Smellie's address!' said Bets joyfully, pleased at having something real to do. 'I'll bring the telephone book out here to Fatty.'

The children were called in to tea, and ran indoors to wash. They were soon sitting down eating bread and butter and jam. Larry and Daisy stayed to tea, but Fatty had to go back to the hotel, as his mother was expecting him.

After tea Fatty came back and joined Bets. Larry and Pip and Daisy got out bicycles and cycled off. They knew the way to Wilmer Green quite well.

'What excuse shall we make for asking to see Horace Peeks?' said Larry, as they cycled quickly along.

Nobody could think of a good excuse. Then Pip had an idea. 'Let's go to the house and just ask for a drink of water,' he said. 'If Mr Peeks's mother is there I expect she'll talk nineteen to the dozen, and we may find out what we want to know – which is – where was Horace Peeks on the evening of the fire? If his mother says he was at home with her all the evening we can cross him off.'

'Good idea!' said Larry. 'And I'll tell you what I'll do, too; just before we get to the house I'll let the air out of my front tyre, see – and pumping up the bike will make a further excuse for staying and talking.'

'Right!' said Pip. 'I do think we are getting clever.'

After cycling for some time they came to the village of Wilmer Green. It was a pretty place, with a duck-pond on which many white ducks were swimming. The children got off their bicycles and began to look for Ivy Cottage. They asked a little girl where it was, and she pointed it out to them. It was well set back from the road, and backed on to a wood.

The children rode to it, dismounted and went in

to the old wooden gate. Larry had already let the air out of his front tyre and it was almost flat.

'I'll ask for the water,' said Daisy. They went up to the door, which was half open. There was the sound of an iron going thump, thump, thump.

Daisy knocked on the door. 'Who's there?' said a sharp voice.

'Please could we have a drink of water?' asked Daisy.

'Come in and get it,' said the voice. Daisy opened the door wide and went in. She saw a sharp-faced old lady ironing a shirt. She nodded her head towards a tap over a sink.

'Water's there,' she said. 'Cup's on the shelf behind.'

The two boys came in whilst Daisy was running the water. 'Good evening,' they said politely. 'Thank you so much for letting us have some water. We've cycled quite a way, and we're awfully hot,' said Larry. The old lady looked at him approvingly. He was a good-looking boy, and had beautiful manners when he liked.

'Where have you come from?' she asked, thumping with her iron.

'From Peterswood,' said Larry. 'I don't expect you know it, do you?'

'That I do,' said the old lady. 'My son was in service there with a Mr Hick.'

'Oh, how funny!' said Daisy, sipping the cup of water. 'We were down in Mr Hick's garden the other night, when there was a fire.'

'A fire!' said the old woman, startled. 'What fire? I hadn't heard anything of that. Not Mr Hick's house, surely?'

'No – only his cottage workroom,' said Pip. 'No one was hurt. But surely your son would have told you about it, wouldn't he – didn't he see it?'

'When was the fire?' asked the old lady.

Pip told her. Mrs Peeks stopped ironing and thought. 'Well, now, that was the day Horace came home,' she said. 'That's why he didn't know anything about it. He'd had a quarrel with Mr Hick, and he gave notice. He got here in the afternoon and gave me a real start.'

'Then he must have missed the fire,' said Pip. 'I expect he was with you all the evening, wasn't he?'

'No, he wasn't,' said Mrs Peeks. 'He went out after tea on his bike, and I didn't see him again till it was dark. I didn't ask him where he went. I'm not one for poking and prying. I expect he was down at the Pig and Whistle, playing darts. He's a rare one for darts, is our Horace.'

The children exchanged glances. So Horace disappeared after tea – and didn't come back till dark! That seemed very suspicious indeed. *Very* suspicious! Where was he that evening? It would have been so easy to slip back to Peterswood on his bike, hide in the ditch, and set fire to the cottage when no one was about – and then cycle back unseen in the darkness!

Larry wondered what sort of shoes Horace wore. He looked round the kitchen. There was a pair of shoes waiting to be cleaned in a corner. They were about the size of the footprint. But they didn't have rubber soles. Perhaps Mr Peeks was wearing them now. The children wished he would come in.

'I must just go and pump up my front tyre,' said Larry, getting up. 'I won't be a minute.'

But although he left the other two quite five minutes to talk, there didn't seem anything more to be found out. They said good-bye to Mrs Peeks and went to join Larry.

'Didn't find out anything else,' said Pip in a low voice. 'Hello – who's this? Do you think it is Horace?'

They saw a weedy-looking young man coming in at the gate. He had an untidy lock of hair that hung over his forehead, a weak chin, and rather bulging blue eyes, a little like Mr Goon's. He wore a grey flannel coat!

All the children noticed this immediately. Daisy's heart began to beat fast. Could they have found the right person at last?

'What you doing here?' asked Horace Peeks.

'We came to ask for a drink of water,' said Larry, wondering if he could possibly edge round Horace to see if there was a tear in his grey coat anywhere!

'And we found out that we come from the same place that you lived in only a little while ago,' said Daisy brightly. 'We live at Peterswood.'

'That's where I worked,' said Horace. 'Do you know that bad-tempered old Mr Hick? I worked for him, but nothing was ever right. Nasty old man.'

'We don't like him very much ourselves,' said Pip. 'Did you know there was a fire at his place the day you left?'

'How do you know what day I left?' asked Mr Peeks, astonished.

'Oh, we just mentioned the fire to your mother and she said it must have been the day you left, because you didn't know anything about it,' said Pip.

'Well, all I can say is that Mr Hick deserved to have his whole place burnt down, the mean, stingy, bad-tempered old fish!' said Horace. 'I'd like to have seen it!'

The children looked at him, wondering if he was pretending or not. 'Weren't you there, then?' asked Daisy, in an innocent voice.

'Never you mind where I was!' said Peeks. He looked round at Larry, who was edging all round him to see if he could spot a tear in the grey flannel coat that Horace was wearing. 'What are you doing?' he asked. 'Sniffing round me like a dog! Stop it!'

'You've got a spot on your coat,' said Larry, making up the first excuse he could think of. 'I'll rub it off.'

He pulled out his handkerchief – and with it came the letter that Lily had given to him to give to Horace Peeks! It fell to the ground, address side upwards! Horace bent to pick it up and stared in the utmost astonishment at his own name on the envelope!

He turned to Larry. 'What's this?' he said.

Larry could have kicked himself for his carelessness. 'Oh, it's for you,' he said. 'Lily asked us to post it to you, but as we were coming over here we thought we might as well deliver it by hand.'

Horace Peeks looked as if he was going to ask some awkward questions, and Larry thought it was about time to go. He wheeled his bicycle to the gate.

'Well, good-bye,' he said. 'I'll tell Lily you've got her letter.'

The three of them mounted their bicycles and rode off. Horace shouted after them. 'Hey! You come back a minute!'

But they didn't go back. Their minds were in a whirl! They rode for about a mile and a half, and then Larry jumped off his bicycle and went to sit on a gate. 'Come on!' he called to the others. 'We'll just talk a bit and see what we think.'

They sat in a row on the gate, looking very serious. 'I was an idiot to drag that letter out of my pocket like that,' said Larry, looking ashamed of himself. 'But perhaps it was as well. I suppose letters ought to be delivered – oughtn't they? Do you think Horace started the fire?'

'It looks rather like it,' said Daisy thoughtfully. 'He had a spite against Mr Hick that very day, and his mother doesn't know where he was that night. You didn't notice if his shoes had rubber, criss-crossed soles, did you, Larry? And was his grey flannel coat torn in any way?'

'I couldn't see his shoe soles, and as far as I could see, his coat wasn't torn at all,' said Larry. 'Anyway, that letter will warn him now, and he'll be on his guard!'

They talked for a little while, wondering what to do about Mr Peeks. They decided that they would set him aside for a while and see what Mr Smellie was like. It seemed to rest now between Horace Peeks and Mr Smellie. It was no good deciding about Mr Peeks until they had also seen Mr Smellie!

They mounted their bicycles again and set off. They freewheeled down a hill and round a corner. Larry went into someone with a crash! He fell off and so did the other person!

Larry sat up and stared apologetically at the man

in the road. To his horror it was old Clear-Orf!

'What! You again!' yelled Mr Goon, in a most threatening voice. Larry hurriedly got up. The other two were farther down the road, laughing.

'What you doing?' yelled Mr Goon, as Larry stood his bicycle upright, ready to mount again.

'I'm clearing orf!' shouted Larry. 'Can't you see? I'm clearing orf!'

And the three of them rode giggling down the hill, pausing to wonder every now and again if old Clear-Orf was on his way to see Horace Peeks! Well – Horace was now warned by Lily's letter – so Mr Goon wouldn't get much out of him, that was certain!

11. THE TRAMP TURNS UP AGAIN

It was seven o'clock when the three of them rode up Pip's drive. Bets was getting worried, because her bedtime was coming very near, and she couldn't bear to think that she would have to go before she heard the news that Larry, Daisy and Pip might be bringing.

She jumped for joy when she heard their bicycle bells jangling as they rode at top speed up the drive. It was such a lovely evening that she, Fatty and Buster were still in the garden. Fatty had examined his bruises again, and was pleased to see that they were now a marvellous red-purple. Although they hurt him he couldn't help being very proud of them.

'What news? What news?' yelled Bets, as the three travellers returned.

'Plenty!' cried Larry. 'Half a tick – let's put our bikes away!'

Soon all five and Buster were sitting in the summerhouse talking. Fatty's eyes nearly dropped out of his head when he heard how Larry had dragged the letter out of his pocket and dropped it by accident at Horace Peeks's feet.

'But Clear-Orf's on the trail all right,' said Pip. 'We met him as we were going home. Larry knocked him off his bike, going round the corner. Clear-Orf must be brighter than we think. He's a little way behind us, that's all!'

'Well, we'd better get on Mr Smellie's track as soon as possible tomorrow,' said Fatty. 'Bets and I have got his address.'

'Good for you,' said Larry. 'Where does he live?'

'It was in the telephone book,' said Bets. 'It was very easy to find because there was only one Mr Smellie. He lives at Willow-Dene, Jeffreys Lane.'

'Why, that's just at the back of our garden,' said Larry, in surprise. 'Isn't it, Daisy? Willow-Dene backs on to half our garden. I never knew who lived there, because we've never once seen anyone in the garden, except an old woman.'

'That would be Miss Miggle, the housekeeper,' said Fatty.

'How do you know?' asked Daisy, in surprise.

'Oh, Bets and I have been very good Find-Outers today,' said Fatty, with a grin. 'We asked your gardener where Willow-Dene was, and he knew it, because his brother works there. And he told us about Miss Miggle, and how difficult she finds it to keep old Mr Smellie clean, and make him have his meals, and remember to put his mack on when it rains, and so on.'

'What's the matter with him, then?' said Larry. 'Is he mad or silly or something?'

'Oh no. He's a something-ologist,' said Bets. 'He studies old, old papers and documents, and knows more about them than anyone else. He doesn't care about anything but old writings. The gardener says he's got some very, very valuable ones himself.'

'Well, as he conveniently lives so near us, perhaps Larry and I could interview him tomorrow,' said Daisy, very much looking forward to a bit more Find-Outing, as Bets kept calling it. 'I think we're getting rather good at interviewing. I bet we're better than old Clear-Orf. Any suspect would know at once that Mr Goon was after him and would be careful what he said. But people talk to children without thinking anything about it.'

Larry got his notes out from behind the loose board in the summerhouse. 'We must add a bit to them,' he said, and began to write. Pip got out the match box and opened it. He wanted to see if the bit of grey flannel was at all like the grey coat that Horace Peeks had worn. It did look rather like it.

'Still, Larry couldn't see any torn bit,' said Pip. 'And I had a good look at his trousers too, but I couldn't see any tear in them.'

The children stared at the grey flannel. Pip put it back into the box. He unfolded Fatty's beautiful drawing of the footprints, and grinned as he remembered the tail, ears and hands that he and Larry had so solemnly talked about when they first looked at the footprints in the drawing.

'You know it's not half a bad drawing,' said Pip. Fatty brightened up very much, but he was wise enough not to say a word this time. 'I shall learn these criss-cross markings by heart, so that if ever I come across them at any time I shall know them at once.'

'I'll learn them too,' said Bets, and she stared seriously at the drawing. She felt quite certain that if ever she spotted a footprint anywhere in the mud with those special markings, she would know them immediately.

'I've finished my notes,' said Larry. 'I can't say that our clues have helped us at all. We must really find out if Mr Peeks wears rubber-soled shoes – and we mustn't forget to look at Mr Smellie's either.'

'But they may not be wearing them,' objected Fatty. 'They might have them in the cupboard, or in their bedroom.'

'Perhaps we could peep into Mr Smellie's boot cupboard,' said Larry, who hadn't the faintest idea how he would set about doing such a thing. 'Listen – there are four suspects. One was Mrs Minns, but as she had rheumatism all the evening of the fire, and was stuck in her chair, according to her sister, *she* couldn't have started the fire. So that leaves three suspects. The tramp was another suspect, but as he does not wear rubber-soled shoes, or a grey coat, and did not get away quickly as we might have expected him to, we can practically rule him out too. So that leaves two suspects.'

'I think it was Horace Peeks,' said Pip. 'Why shouldn't he tell us where he was on the evening of the fire? That's very suspicious.'

'Well, if Mr Smellie can tell us where *he* was, that will only leave Horace Peeks,' said Larry. 'Then we will really pay all our attention to him, find out what his shoes are like, and if he has a grey coat indoors with a tear, and what he was doing on that evening and everything.'

'*Then* what do we do?' asked Bets. 'Go and tell the police?'

'What! Tell old Clear-Orf and have him taking all the credit and praise to himself?' cried Larry. 'I should think not. We ought to go to the Inspector of Police himself, Inspector Jenks. He's head of all the police in this district. Daddy knows him quite well. He's a very, very clever man, and he lives in the next town.'

'I should be frightened of him,' said Bets. 'I'm even a bit frightened of Clear-Orf.'

'Pooh! Frightened of that old stick-in-the-mud with his froggy eyes?' said Fatty. 'You want to be like Larry, sail down a hill on your bike and knock him off, crash, round the corner!'

Everyone laughed. Then they were called for dinner and the five got up, with Buster running round their legs. Fatty said goodnight and went to have dinner with his father and mother at the hotel. Larry and Daisy got their bicycles and rode home. Pip went in to supper and Bets went off to bed. Buster went with Fatty.

'Tomorrow that old tramp will come to get the boots Mummy has looked out for him,' said Pip to Bets. 'We'll ask him a few questions.'

'What questions?' asked Bets.

'We'll ask him straight out if he saw Horace Peeks in the ditch, hiding,' said Pip. 'If he says yes, that will be a great help to us.'

None of the children slept very well that night for they were all excited over the happenings of the day. Bets dreamt of Clear-Orf, and woke with a squeal, dreaming that he was putting her in prison for starting the fire! Fatty slept badly because of his bruises. It didn't matter how he lay, he seemed to lie on two or three.

It had been arranged that the next day Pip and Bets and Fatty should stay in their garden, on the look out for the tramp. Pip should question him carefully. Larry had told him what to ask.

'Have the boots out so that he can see them and

want them badly,' said Larry. 'But don't let him have them till he's answered your questions. No answers, no boots. See?'

So the next day Fatty and Buster joined Pip and Bets, and the four of them waited for the tramp to turn up.

The tramp did turn up. He slipped slyly in at the back gate, looking all round and about as if he thought someone was after him. He still had on the terrible old shoes, with toes sticking out of the upper parts. Pip saw him and gave a low call.

'Hello! Come over here!'

The tramp looked over to where Pip was standing. 'You're not setting that bobby after me?' he asked.

'Of course not,' said Pip impatiently. 'We don't like him any more than you do.'

'Got the boots?' asked the tramp. Pip nodded. The old fellow shambled over to him and Pip took him to the summerhouse. There was a small wooden table there, and the boots were on it. The tramp's eyes gleamed when he saw them.

'Good boots,' he said. 'They'll fit me proper.'

'Wait a minute,' said Pip, as the tramp put out

his hand to take them. 'Wait a minute. We want you to answer a few questions first, please.'

The tramp stared at him, and looked sulky. 'I'm not going to be mixed up in no trouble,' he said.

'Of course not,' said Pip. 'We shan't split on you. What you tell us we shall keep to ourselves.'

'What do you want to know?' asked the tramp.

'Did you see anyone hiding in Mr Hick's garden on the evening of the fire?' asked Fatty.

'Yes,' said the tramp. 'I saw someone in the bushes.'

Bets, Pip and Fatty felt quite breathless. 'Did you really *see* them?' asked Pip.

'Course I see them,' said the tramp. 'I see plenty of people in the garden that evening, so I did.'

'Where were you?' asked Bets curiously.

'That's none of your business,' said the tramp roughly. 'I wasn't doing no harm.'

'Probably watching the hen-house, waiting for a chance of an egg or two, even though old Hiccup had chased him away,' thought Pip, quite correctly.

They all stared at the tramp, and he stared back. 'Was the person who was hiding in the bushes a young man, with a lock of hair falling over his forehead?' asked Pip, describing Horace Peeks. 'Did he have sort of bulgy eyes?'

'Don't know about his eyes,' said the tramp. 'But he had a lock of hair all right. He was whispering to someone, but I couldn't see who.'

This was news. Horace Peeks hiding in the bushes with somebody else! Were there two people concerned in the crime then?

It was a puzzle. Could Horace Peeks and Mr Smellie have planned the fire together? The children didn't know what to think.

'Look here,' began Pip. But the tramp had had enough.

'You give me them boots,' he said, and he stretched out his hand for them. 'I'm not saying no more. Be getting myself into trouble if I don't look out. I don't want to be mixed up in anything, I don't. I'm a very honest fellow.'

He took the boots and put them on. He would not say a word more. 'He seems to have gone dumb,' said Pip. They watched the tramp walk away in his new boots, which were a little too big for him, but otherwise very comfortable.

'Well, the mystery is getting deeper,' said Fatty.

'Now we seem to have *two* people hiding in the garden, instead of one. There's no doubt one was dear Horace. But who was the other? Perhaps Larry and Daisy will have some news for us when they come.'

Buster had growled nearly all the time the tramp had been in the summerhouse. Fatty had had to hold him tight, or he would have flown at the dirty old fellow. Now he suddenly began to bark joyously.

'It's Larry and Daisy,' said Bets. 'Oh, good. I wonder if they've got any news.'

12. MR SMELLIE – AND A RUBBER-SOLED SHOE

Larry and Daisy had spent an exciting morning. They had decided to interview old Mr Smellie as soon as possible, and get it over. They talked over the best way of tackling him.

'We can't very well go and ask for a drink of water or anything like that,' said Daisy. 'I simply can't imagine what excuse we can make up for going to see him.'

They both thought hard for some minutes. Then Larry looked up. 'What about throwing our ball into Mr Smellie's garden?' he said.

'What good would that do?' asked Daisy.

'Well, silly, we could go after it – climb over the wall, don't you see – and hope that he will see us and ask what we're doing,' said Larry.

'I see,' said Daisy. 'Yes – it seems quite a good idea. We'll do that.'

So Larry threw his ball high and it went over the

trees, and fell in the middle of the lawn next door. The children ran down to the wall at the bottom. In a moment or two they were over it and in the bushes at the end of Mr Smellie's garden.

They went boldly out on to the lawn and began hunting for the ball. They could see it quite well, for it was in the edge of a rose-bed on the lawn. They called to one another as they hunted, hoping that someone in the house would hear them and come to a window.

Presently a window opened at the right side of the house, and a man looked out. His head was quite bald on top, and he had a straggling beard that reached almost to the middle of his waistcoat. He wore heavy horn-rimmed glasses that made his eyes look very big.

'What are you doing?' he called.

Larry went and stood under the window and spoke extremely politely.

'I hope you don't mind, sir, but our ball fell in your garden, and we're looking for it.'

A gust of wind blew into the garden and flung Daisy's hair over her face. It tugged at Mr Smellie's beard, and it rustled round the papers on the desk by him. One of them rose into the air and flew straight out of the window. Mr Smellie made a grab at it, but didn't catch it. It fell to the ground below.

'I'll get it for you, sir,' said Larry politely. He picked up the paper and handed it back to the old man.

'What a very peculiar paper,' he said. It was thick and yellow, and covered with curious writing.

'It is parchment,' said Mr Smellie, looking at Larry out of short-sighted eyes. 'This is very, very old.'

Larry thought it would be a good idea to take a great interest in old papers. 'Oh, sir!' he said. 'Is it really very old? How old? How very interesting!'

Mr Smellie was pleased to have anyone taking such a sudden interest. 'I have much older ones,' he said. 'I spend my time deciphering them – reading them, you know. We learn a great deal of old history that way.'

'How marvellous!' said Larry. 'I suppose you couldn't show me any, sir, could you?'

'Certainly, my boy, certainly,' said Mr Smellie, positively beaming at Larry. 'Come along in. I think you will find that the garden door is open.'

'Could my sister come too?' asked Larry. 'She would be very, very interested, I know.'

Dear me, what unusual children, thought Mr Smellie, as he watched them going in at the garden door. They were just wiping their feet when a little bird-like woman darted out of a room nearby and gazed at them in surprise.

'Whatever are you doing here?' she said. 'This is Mr Smellie's house. He doesn't allow anyone inside.'

'He's just asked us in,' said Larry politely. 'We have wiped our feet very carefully.'

'Just asked you in!' said Miss Miggle, the house-keeper, filled with astonishment. 'But he never asks *any*one in – except Mr Hick. And since they quarrelled even he hasn't been here.'

'But perhaps Mr Smellie has visited Mr Hick!' said Larry, still wiping his feet, anxious to go on with the conversation.

'No, indeed he hasn't,' said Miss Miggle. 'He told me that he wasn't going to visit any one who shouted at him in the disgusting way that Mr Hick did. Poor old gentleman, he doesn't deserve to be shouted at. He's very absent-minded and a bit odd sometimes, but there's no harm in him.'

124

'Didn't he go down and see the fire when Mr Hick's workroom got burnt?' asked Daisy. Miss Miggle shook her head.

'He went out for his usual walk that evening,' she said. 'About six o'clock. But he came back before the fire was discovered.'

The children looked at one another. So Mr Smellie had gone out that evening – could he possibly have slipped down to Mr Hick's, started the fire and come back again?

'Did you see the fire?' asked the housekeeper, with interest. But the children had no time to answer, for Mr Smellie came out to see what they were doing. They went with him into his study – a most untidy room, strewn with all kinds of papers, its walls lined with books that reached right up to the ceiling.

'Gracious!' said Daisy, looking round. 'Doesn't anyone ever tidy this room? You can hardly walk without stepping on papers!'

'Miss Miggle is forbidden to tidy this room,' said Mr Smellie, putting his glasses on firmly. They had a habit of slipping down his nose, which was rather small. 'Now let me show you these old, old books –

written on rolls of paper – in the year, let me see now, in the year . . . er, er . . . I must look it up again. I knew it quite well, but that fellow Hick always contradicts me, and he muddles my mind so that I can't remember.'

'I expect your quarrel a day or two ago really upset you,' said Daisy, most sympathetically. Mr Smellie took off his glasses, polished them and put them back on his nose again.

'Yes,' he said, 'yes. I don't like quarrels. Hick is a most intelligent fellow, but he gets very angry if I don't always agree with him. Now *this* document . . .'

The children listened patiently, not under-standing a word of all the long speech that Mr Smellie was making. He quite forgot that he was talking to children, and he spoke as if Larry and Daisy were as learned as himself. They began to feel very bored. When he turned to get another sheaf of old papers, Larry whispered to Daisy, 'Go and see if you can find any of his shoes in the cupboard outside in the hall.'

Daisy slipped out. Mr Smellie didn't seem to notice that she was gone. Larry thought he would hardly notice if he, Larry, went too!

Daisy found the hall cupboard. She opened the door and went inside. It was full of boots, shoes, sticks and coats. Daisy hurriedly looked at the shoes. She turned up each pair. They seemed about the right size, but they hadn't rubber soles.

Then she turned up a pair that *had* rubber soles! How marvellous! Perhaps they were the very ones! She looked at the markings – but for the life of her she couldn't quite remember the markings in the drawing of the footprint. Where they or were they not just like the ones she was looking at?

I'll have to compare them, thought the girl at last. I must take one shoe home with me and go down to see the footprint drawing. We shall soon see if they are the right ones.

She stuffed a shoe up the front of her jersey. It made a very funny lump, but she couldn't think where else to hide the shoe. She crept out of the hall cupboard – straight into Miss Miggle!

Miss Miggle was tremendously astonished to see Daisy coming out of the boot cupboard. 'Whatever are you doing?' she asked. 'Surely you are not playing hide-and-seek?'

'Well – not *exactly*,' said Daisy, who didn't quite

know what to say. Miss Miggle carried a tray of buns and milk into the study, where Mr Smellie was still lecturing to poor Larry. She put the tray down on the table. Daisy followed close behind her, hoping that no one would notice the enormous lump up her jersey.

'I thought the children would like to share your eleven o'clock lunch with you, sir,' said Miss Miggle. She turned to look at Daisy. 'Gracious, child – is that your hanky up the front of your jersey. What a place to keep it!'

Larry glanced at his sister and was amazed to see the curious lump behind her jersey.

'I keep all kinds of things up my jersey-front,' said Daisy, hoping that no one would ask her to show what she had. Nobody did. Larry was just about to, but stopped himself in time on seeing that the lump was decidedly the shape of a shoe!

The children had milk and buns, but Mr Smellie did not touch his. Miss Miggle kept at his elbow, trying to stop him talking and to make him eat and drink.

'You have your milk now, sir,' she kept saying. 'You didn't have your breakfast, you know.' She turned to the children. 'Ever since the night of the fire poor Mr Smellie has been terribly upset. Haven't you, sir?'

'Well, the loss of those unique and quite irreplaceable documents in the fire gave me a shock,' said Mr Smellie. 'Worth thousands of pounds they were. Oh, I know Hick was insured and will get his money back all right, but that isn't the point. The documents were of the greatest imaginable value.'

'Did you quarrel about those that morning?' asked Daisy.

'Oh no; you see, Hick said these documents here, that I've just been showing you, were written by a man called Ulinus,' said Mr Smellie earnestly, 'and I know perfectly well that they were written by three different people. I could not make Mr Hick see reason. He flew into a terrible temper, and practically turned me out of the house. In fact, he really frightened me. He frightened me so much that I left my documents behind.'

'Poor Mr Smellie,' said Daisy. 'I suppose you didn't know anything about the fire till the morning?'

'Not a thing!' said Mr Smellie.

'Didn't you go near Mr Hick's house when you went for your evening walk?' asked Larry. 'If you had, you might have seen the fire starting.'

Mr Smellie looked startled. His glasses fell right off his nose. He picked them up with a trembling hand and put them on again. Miss Miggle put a hand on his arm.

'Now, now,' she said, 'you just drink up your milk, sir. You're not yourself this last day or two. You told me you didn't know where you went that evening. You just wandered about.'

'Yes,' said Mr Smellie, sitting down heavily in a chair. 'That's what I did, didn't I, Miss Miggle? I just wandered about. I can't always remember what I do, can I?'

'No, you can't, sir,' said kind Miss Miggle, patting Mr Smellie's shoulder. 'The quarrel and the fire have properly upset you. Don't you worry, sir!'

She turned to the children and spoke in a low voice. 'You'd better go. He's got himself a bit upset.'

The children nodded and slipped out. They went into the garden, ran down to the bottom and climbed over the wall.

'Funny, isn't it?' said Daisy. 'Why did he act so

strangely when we began to ask him what he did the evening of the fire? Do you suppose he did start it – and has forgotten all about it? Or remembers it and is frightened? Or what?'

'It's a puzzle,' said Larry. 'He seems too gentle a man to do anything so awful as burn a cottage down – but he might be fierce in some odd way. What *have* you got under your jersey, Daisy?'

'A rubber-soled shoe with funny markings,' said Daisy, bringing it out. 'Do you think it is like the footprint?'

'It looks as if it might be,' said Larry, getting excited. 'Let's go straight to the others and compare it with the drawing. Come on! I can hardly wait!'

13. A SURPRISING TALK WITH LILY

Larry and Daisy rushed up to the others. They stared at the shoe in her hand in excitement.

'Daisy! Oh, Daisy! Have you found the rubber-soled shoes that belong to the man who burnt the cottage?' cried Fatty.

'I think so,' said Daisy importantly. 'You see, Larry and I went to see Mr Smellie, as we had planned to do – and whilst he was talking to Larry I slipped away and looked in his hall cupboard where shoes and things are kept. And among the shoes I found one pair that had rubber soles – and I'm almost certain the markings are the same as in those footprints we saw.'

The children crowded round to look. 'It certainly looks very like the right shoe,' said Pip.

'It *is*,' said Fatty. 'I ought to know, because I drew the prints!'

'Well, *I* don't think it is,' said Bets unexpectedly.

'The squares on the criss-cross pattern aren't quite so big. I'm sure they're not.'

'As if *you* could tell!' said Pip scornfully. 'I think we've got the right shoe – and we'll prove it. Get the drawing out of the summerhouse, Fatty.'

Fatty went to get it. He took it from behind the loose board and brought it out to the others. They unfolded it, feeling very thrilled.

They all gazed at the drawing, and then at the underneath of Mr Smellie's shoe. They looked very, very hard indeed, and then they sighed in disappointment.

'Bets is right,' said Fatty. 'The squares in the pattern of the rubber sole are not quite so big as in my drawing. And I know my drawing is quite correct, because I measured everything carefully. I'm awfully good at things like that. I never make . . .'

'Shut up,' said Larry, who always felt cross when Fatty began his boasting. 'Bets, as you say, is quite right. Good for you, young Bets!'

Bets glowed with pleasure. She really *had* learnt that drawing off by heart, as she had said she would. But she was as disappointed as the others that Daisy had not found the right shoe after all.

'It's awfully difficult being a Find-Outer, isn't it?' said Bets. 'We keep finding out things that aren't much help, or that make everything even more difficult. Pip, tell Larry and Daisy what the tramp said.'

'Oh yes – you must hear about that,' said Pip; and he began to tell Larry and Daisy what had happened with the tramp.

'So now, you see, it's a bigger puzzle than ever,' finished Pip. 'The tramp saw Mr Peeks all right, hiding in the bushes – but he heard him whispering to someone else! Was it old Mr Smellie, do you think? You say that he went out for a walk that evening, and we know that Mr Peeks was out at that time too. Do you suppose they planned the fire together?'

'They might have,' said Larry thoughtfully. 'They must have known one another – and they might have got together that day and made up their minds to punish old Hiccup for his unkindness. However can we find out?'

'Perhaps we had better see Mr Smellie again?' said Daisy. 'Anyway, we must put back his shoe somehow. We can't keep it. Anyone seen Clear-Orf today?'

Nobody had, and nobody wanted to. The children talked over what they were to do next. At the moment everything seemed rather muddled and difficult. Although they had ruled out Mrs Minns and the tramp from their list of suspects, it seemed impossible to know whether Mr Peeks or Mr Smellie, or both, had really done the crime.

'It wouldn't be a bad idea to go and see Lily,' said Fatty suddenly. 'She might tell us a few things about Horace Peeks. After all, she wrote him a letter to warn him. She might know more than we think!'

'But Lily wasn't there that evening,' said Daisy. 'It was her evening off. She said so.'

'Well, how are we to know she didn't go back to Hiccup's and hide in the garden?' said Fatty.

'It seems as if half the village was hiding in that garden on the evening of the fire,' said Larry. 'The old tramp was there – and we think Mr Smellie was – and we know Mr Peeks was – and now you say perhaps Lily was too!'

'I know. It's really funny to think how full

Hiccup's garden was that evening!' grinned Fatty. 'Well – don't you think it would be a good thing to go and see Lily? I don't suspect *her* of anything – but it would be just as well to see if she can tell us anything to help us.'

'Yes – it's quite a good idea,' said Larry. 'Blow, it's lunchtime, Pip. We'll have to leave things till this afternoon. We'll all go down and see Lily – we'll take something for the cat and kittens again. And what about Mr Smellie's shoe? When shall we take that back?'

'We'd better take it back this evening,' said Daisy. 'You take it back, Larry, when it's dark. You may find the garden door open, and you can just slip in and put the shoe back.'

'Right,' said Larry, and he got up to go. 'We'll be back after lunch, Find-Outers.'

Pip and Bets were running to the house, afraid of getting into trouble if they waited any longer. Fatty went off with Buster.

They all met together again at half-past two. Daisy had stopped at the fishmonger's and bought some fish for the cats. It smelt very strong, and Buster kept worrying her to undo the paper.

'Come on – let's get going. We'd better get off quickly, or it will be teatime before we've finished talking,' said Fatty.

So they set off down the lane to find Lily. They felt certain they would not be caught by Hiccup this time because Pip had seen him go by in his car not long before.

'One or two of us must talk to Mrs Minns,' said Larry, 'and the others had better try and get Lily out into the garden and talk to her. We'll see how things go.'

But, as it happened, everything was very easy. Mrs Minns was out, and there was no one in the kitchen but Lily. She was pleased to see the children and Buster.

'I'll just put Sweetie and the kittens out in the hall, and shut the door,' she said. 'Then that little dog can come in. I like dogs. What's his name? Buster! That's a nice name for a dog. Buster! Buster! Would you like a bone?'

Soon the cat and kittens were safely out of the way and Buster was gnawing a bone on the floor. Lily got out some chocolate from a drawer and handed it round. The children liked her. She seemed much more cheerful without Mrs Minns to shout at her.

'We gave that note to Horace Peeks,' said Larry. 'We found him all right.'

'Yes, I got a letter from him today,' said Lily. She looked rather sad suddenly. 'That nasty Mr Goon went up and saw him and said all kinds of horrible things to him. Horace is that worried he doesn't know what to do.'

'Did Mr Goon think he had started the fire, then?' asked Daisy.

'Yes,' said Lily. 'A good many people are saying that. But it isn't true.'

'How do you know?' asked Fatty.

'Well, I *do* know,' said Lily.

'But you weren't here,' said Larry. 'If you weren't here, you can't possibly know who did or didn't start the fire. It *might* have been Horace for all you know.'

'Now, don't you say a word if I tell you something, will you?' said Lily suddenly. 'Promise? Say, "Honour bright, I'll not tell a soul." '

The five children recited the seven words very solemnly, and Lily looked relieved.

'Well, then,' she said, 'I'll tell you how I know

it wasn't Horace that did it. I know because I met him at five o'clock that day, and I was with him till I got in here at ten o'clock, which is my time for being in!'

The five children stared at her. This was indeed news.

'But why didn't you tell everyone that?' asked Larry, at last. 'If you said that, no one would say that Horace burnt down the cottage.'

Lily's eyes filled with tears. 'Well, you see,' she said, 'my mother says I'm too young to say I'll marry anyone, but Horace Peeks, he loves me, and I love him. My father said he'd punish me if he caught me walking out with Horace, and Mrs Minns said she'd tell my father if ever she caught me speaking a word to him. So I didn't dare to go out to the pictures with him, or even to talk to him in the house.'

'Poor Lily,' said Daisy. 'So when you heard everyone talking against him, you were very upset and wrote to warn him?'

'Yes,' said Lily. 'And, you see, if I tell that I was out with him that night, my father will punish me, and maybe Mrs Minns will send me off, so

I'll lose my job. And Horace can't say he was with me because he knows it will be hard for me if he does.'

'Where did you go?' asked Fatty.

'I went on my bicycle half-way to Wilmer Green,' said Lily. 'We met at his sister's there and had tea together, and a bite of supper. We told his sister all about how poor Horace had lost his job that day, and she said maybe her husband would give him some work till he could find another job.'

Fatty remembered that the tramp had seen Horace Peeks in the garden that evening, and he looked sharply at Lily. Could she be telling all the truth?

'Are you sure that Horace didn't come here at all that night?' he said. The others knew why he said it – they too remembered that the tramp had said he had seen Horace Peeks.

'No, no!' cried Lily, raising her voice in fright. She twisted her handkerchief round and round in her hands, and stared at the children. 'Horace wasn't anywhere near here. I tell you, we met at his sister's. You can ask her. She'll tell you.'

Larry felt certain that Lily was frightened and

was not telling the truth. He decided to be bold.

'Lily,' he said, in a very solemn voice, '*some*body saw Horace in the garden that evening.'

Lily stared at Larry with wide, horrified eyes. 'No!' she said. 'They couldn't have seen him. They couldn't!'

'Well, they did,' said Larry. Lily stared at him for a moment, and then began to sob.

'Who could have seen him?' she said. 'Mrs Minns and her sister were here in the kitchen. Mr Hick and the chauffeur were out. There wasn't anyone about; I know there wasn't.'

'How do you know, if you weren't here?' asked Larry.

'Well,' said Lily, swallowing a sob. 'Well, I'll tell you. I *was* here! Now don't you forget you've said honour bright you won't tell a soul! You see, this is what happened. I rode off to meet Horace, and when I met him he told me he'd left some of his things at Mr Hick's, and he wanted them. But he didn't dare to go and ask Mr Hick for them. So I said to him, "Well, Horace," I said, "Mr Hick's out, and why don't you come along and get them now, before he comes back?" '

The children listened breathlessly. They were getting the truth at last!

Lily went on, twisting her handkerchief round and round all the time. 'So when we'd had a cup of tea, we rode off here, and we left our bikes behind the hedge up the lane. Nobody saw us. We walked down, behind the hedge, till we got to Mr Hick's. Then we both slipped into the bushes and waited a bit to see if anyone was about.'

The children nodded. The tramp had said that he had heard Mr Peeks whispering to someone – and that someone must have been Lily!

'I soon found out that Mrs Minns had got her sister talking to her,' went on Lily, 'and I knew they'd sit there for ages. I said to Horace that I'd get his things for him if he liked, but he wanted to get them himself. So I kept watch whilst he slipped into the house by an open window, got his things and came out into the bushes again. Then we went off on our bikes, without seeing a soul.'

'And Horace didn't slip down the garden to the workroom?' asked Larry.

Lily looked indignant. 'That he didn't!' she said.

142

'For one thing I'd have seen him. For another thing, he wasn't gone more than three minutes. And for another thing, my Horace wouldn't do a thing like that!'

'Well – that lets Horace out,' said Larry, saying aloud what everyone else was thinking. 'He couldn't have done it. I'm glad you told us all this, Lily. Golly – I do wonder who did it then?'

'It only leaves Mr Smellie,' said Bets, without thinking.

Bets's words had an astonishing result. Lily let out a squeal, and stared at Bets as if she couldn't believe her ears. She opened and shut her mouth like a fish, and didn't seem able to say a word.

'Whatever's the matter?' asked Larry, in surprise.

'What did she say that for?' asked Lily, almost in a whisper. 'How does she know that Mr Smellie was here that night?'

Now it was the children's turn to look surprised. 'Well,' said Larry, 'we don't know for certain. We only just wondered. But why are you so astonished, Lily? What do *you* know about it, anyway? You didn't see Mr Smellie, did you? You said that no one saw you and Horace.'

'That's right,' said Lily. 'But *Horace* saw someone! When he got in through the window, and went upstairs to get his things, he saw someone creeping in through the garden door. And it was Mr Smellie!'

'Golly!' said Larry and Pip. They all stared at one another. 'So Mr Smellie *did* go down here that night!' said Larry.

'No wonder he was so startled when you asked him if he went anywhere near Mr Hick's on the evening of the fire,' said Daisy.

'*He* did it!' said Bets trumphantly. 'Now we know. *He* did it! He's a wicked old man.'

'Do you think he did it?' Fatty asked Lily. She looked puzzled and perplexed.

'*I* don't know,' she said. 'He's a nice, quiet old gentleman, *I* think, and always had a kind word for me. It's not like him to do such a violent thing as set something on fire. But what I *do* know is – it wasn't Horace.'

'No – it doesn't look as if it could have been Horace,' agreed Larry. 'I see now why you didn't say anything before, Lily – you were afraid. Well, we shan't tell anyone. It seems to me that we must now turn more of our attention to Mr Smellie!'

'No doubt about that!' said Fatty. 'Well – we've certainly found out a few things this afternoon!'

14. CLEAR-ORF TURNS UP AT AN AWKWARD MOMENT

The children stayed talking to Lily for a little while, and then, as it was getting near teatime they had to go. The girl was relieved to have told somebody of her troubles, and she saw them off, after they had once more promised to keep to themselves all that she had told them.

They were all having tea at Pip's, which was nice because they could talk everything over. They were very excited indeed.

'Things are moving!' said Pip, rubbing his hands together. 'They certainly are moving! I don't believe Horace Peeks had anything to do with it at all. Not a thing. I think it was Mr Smellie. Look how scared he was when you and Daisy spoke to him about his walk that evening. Why should he be scared if he hadn't done anything wrong?'

'And we know his shoes are the right size, even

if the rubber soles don't match the drawing,' said Daisy.

'Maybe he *has* got a pair that *do* match,' said Fatty, 'but he's hidden them somewhere in case he did leave footprints behind. He might have thought of that.'

'Yes, that's so,' said Larry. 'If only we could find someone with a torn grey flannel suit – that really would settle matters!'

'We really ought to search and see if we can find those shoes,' said Daisy. 'I should think they are in his study somewhere. You know he told us that Miss Miggle isn't allowed to tidy up in there. He could easily pop them into a cupboard there, or behind those rows of books or somewhere.'

'Daisy, that's a clever idea of yours,' said Larry, pleased. 'I believe you're right. Shall I creep in tonight and have a hunt?'

'Are we allowed to get into people's houses and hunt for their shoes?' said Pip doubtfully.

'Well, we can't ask anybody that,' said Larry. 'We'll just have to do it. We're not doing anything wrong. We're only trying to find out something.'

'I know. But grown-ups are funny,' said Pip. 'I'm

sure most of them wouldn't like children creeping about their houses looking for clues.'

'Well, I don't see what else to do,' said Larry. 'I really don't. Anyway, silly, we've got to put back the shoe that Daisy took, haven't we?'

'Yes,' agreed Pip. 'That certainly must be done. Don't get caught, that's all!'

'I shan't,' said Larry. 'Sh – here comes your mother, Pip. Talk about something else.'

Pip's mother asked Fatty how he was after his fall.

'Thank you, I'm all right,' he said, 'but I've still got some nasty bruises.

Leaving Fatty talking eagerly to Pip's mother, the four children crept off. Buster stayed with Fatty, wagging his tail.

'Let's go for a bike ride and leave old Fatty to himself,' said Pip, in disgust. 'I don't want to hear about his fall all over again.'

So the four of them went for a bike ride and Fatty was surprised and hurt to find that he was all alone in the garden, when Pip's mother left him. He couldn't think why the others had gone, and he spent a miserable hour by himself, thinking how unkind they were.

When they came back, he greeted them with a volley of complaints.

'You *are* mean! Why did you go off like that? Is that the way to behave, Pip, when people come to tea with you? You're horrid!'

'Well, we thought you'd probably be about an hour boasting to Pip's mother,' said Larry. 'Don't look so fierce, Fatty. You shouldn't be such an idiot!'

'Going off like that finding clues and things without me,' said Fatty angrily. 'Aren't I a Find-Outer too? What have you been doing? Seeing Horace Peeks – or Lily again? You *are* mean!'

'We didn't see anyone,' said Bets, feeling sorry for Fatty. She had so often been left out of things because she was younger than the others, and she knew how horrid it was to feel left out. 'We only went for a bike ride.'

But Fatty was really offended and hurt. 'I don't think I want to belong to the Find-Outers any more,' he said. 'I'll take my drawing of the foot-prints and go. I can see you don't want me. Come on, Buster.'

Nobody wanted Buster to leave the Find-Outers

– and they didn't really want Fatty to, either. He wasn't so bad once you got used to him.

Daisy went after him. 'Come back, silly,' she said. 'We do want you. We want to discuss what to do tonight about Mr Smellie's shoes. You come and say what we ought to do, too. I want to go into Mr Smellie's house and keep guard for Larry, whilst he is hunting for the shoes we think Mr Smellie has hidden. But he won't let me.'

Fatty went back to the others, still looking rather sulky.

'Larry, I do wish you'd let me creep into Mr Smellie's house with you,' said Daisy. 'Fatty, don't you think I really ought to keep guard for him?'

'No, I don't,' said Fatty. 'I think I ought to go with Larry. You shall do the hunting and I'll watch out that nobody discovers you.'

'No, I'll go,' said Pip, at once.

'You wouldn't be able to slip out without being seen,' said Larry. 'Fatty could. His parents don't seem to bother about him much. All right, Fatty – you come and help me then. I thought I'd wait till about half past nine, and then scout about and see if old Smellie is still in his study. It's no use trying anything till he's gone to bed. He may be one of these people that stays up till about three o'clock in the morning, of course. We'll have to see.'

'Well, I'll be along about half past nine,' said Fatty. 'Where's the shoe? In the summerhouse? I'll bring it with me, in case your mother wants to know where you got it from. It'll be dark then and no one will see what I'm carrying.'

Fatty cheered up very much when he found that there was something really exciting he could join in. He forgot his sulks, and discussed where to meet Larry.

'I shall climb over the wall at the bottom of the garden,' said Larry. 'But you, Fatty, had better go up the road in front of Mr Smellie's house, and go into the drive there, and round to the back that way. Meet me somewhere at the back of the house. See?'

'Right,' said Fatty. 'I'll hoot like an owl to tell you when I'm there.'

'Can you hoot?' said Bets, in surprise.

'Yes, listen,' said Fatty. He put his two thumbs side by side, frontways, and cupped his hands together. He blew carefully between his thumbs, and at once a mournful quavering hoot, just like an owl's, came from his closed hands. It was marvellous.

'Oh, you *are* clever, Fatty!' said Bets, in great admiration. Fatty blew again, and an owl's hoot sounded over the garden. He really was very good at it.

'Simply wonderful!' said Bets. Fatty opened his mouth to say that he could make much better bird and animal noises than that, but caught a look in Larry's eye that warned him in time to say nothing. He shut his mouth again hurriedly.

'Well,' said Larry, 'that's settled then. You meet me at half past nine behind Mr Smellie's house, and hoot like an owl to tell me you're there. I shall probably be hiding in the bushes somewhere, waiting for you.'

The children all felt excited as they went to bed that night. At least, Fatty didn't go to bed, though Larry did. But then Larry's mother usually came to tuck him up and say goodnight, and Fatty's didn't. So Fatty felt quite safe as he sat, fully dressed, in his bedroom, reading a book to make the time pass.

At ten past nine he switched off his light and put

his nose outside his bedroom door. There was no one about. He slipped along the passage and down the stairs. Out of the garden door he went, and into the hotel garden. In half a minute he was in the lane, and running up it with the shoe tucked under his coat.

At just before half past nine he came to Mr Smellie's house, and stopped outside the front gate. The house was quite dark. Fatty walked up and down outside for a moment or two to make quite certain that there was no one about.

He didn't see someone standing quite still by one of the big trees that lined the road. He walked down in front of the house once more, making up his mind to go into the drive – and then quite suddenly he felt a strong hand on his shoulder!

Poor Fatty almost jumped out of his skin. 'Oooh!' he said, frightened, and the shoe dropped from beneath his coat!

'Ho!' said a voice that Fatty knew only too well. 'Ho!' A torch was flashed into his face, and the voice said, 'Ho!' again, this time more loudly.

It was Clear-Orf's voice. He had been standing quietly beside the tree, and had been astonished to see Fatty come up the lane, and walk softly up and down in front of the house. Now he was even more astonished to find that it was 'one of them children!' He bent down and picked up the shoe. He stared at it in the greatest astonishment.

'What's this?' he said.

'It looks like a shoe,' said Fatty. 'Let me go! You've no right to clutch me like that.'

'What are you doing with this shoe?' asked Clear-Orf, in an astonished voice. 'Where's the other?'

'I don't exactly know,' said Fatty truthfully.

'None of your cheek,' he said. He turned the shoe upside down and saw the rubber sole. At once the same thought flashed across his mind as had flashed across Daisy's when she had first seen it – the markings were like those on the footprint!

Mr Goon stared at the shoe in amazement. He flashed his torch at Fatty again. 'Where did you get this?' he asked. 'Whose is it?'

Fatty looked obstinate. 'Someone found it and gave it to me,' he said at last.

'I shall keep it for the time being,' said Mr Goon. 'Now you just come-alonga me for a minute.'

But Fatty didn't mean to do that. With a sudden

quick twist he was out of Clear-Orf's grasp and tearing up the lane as fast as he could go. He went right to the top, and then round and into the lane in which Larry's house stood. He slipped into Larry's drive when he came to it and made his way to the bottom of the garden, his heart beating loudly. He shinned up to the top of the wall and dropped down. He made his way cautiously to the back of the house.

Then he hooted like an owl. 'Oooo-oo! Oooo-ooo-ooo-OOOOO!'

15. A FRIGHT FOR LARRY AND FATTY

In another moment poor Fatty almost jumped out of his skin again! Someone clutched his arm hard. He had been expecting an answering whistle or hoot from somewhere about, but he had not guessed that Larry was behind the bush that he himself was standing by.

'Oooh!' said Fatty, startled.

'Sh!' came Larry's voice in a whisper. 'Have you got the shoe?'

'No,' said Fatty, and explained quickly what had happened to it. Larry listened in dismay.

'You *are* an idiot!' he said. 'Giving one of our best clues away to old Clear-Orf like that! He'll know we are after the same ideas as he is now!'

'The shoe wasn't a clue,' argued Fatty. 'It was a mistake. We thought it was a clue, but it wasn't. Anyway, Clear-Orf's got it, and I really couldn't help it. He nearly got me too. I only just managed to twist away.'

'What shall we do?' asked Larry. 'Shall we go in and hunt now? There's no light in the study. Old Mr Smellie must have gone to bed.'

'Yes, come on,' said Fatty. 'Where's the garden door?'

They soon found it, and to their great delight it was still unlocked. As there was a light from the kitchen, the two boys thought that Miss Miggle was still up. They decided to be very cautious indeed.

They slipped in at the door. Larry led the way to the study where he and Daisy had talked to Mr Smellie that day. 'You'd better stay on guard in the hall,' he said. 'Then if Miss Miggle or Mr Smellie do happen to come along you can warn me at once. I shall open one of the windows of the study if I can do it without making a lot of noise – then I can slip out of it if anyone thinks of walking into the room.'

Larry went into the study. He had a torch with him, and he shone it round the untidy room. There were papers everywhere! Papers and books on the desk, papers and books on the floor and on the chairs. There were books in the bookcases that lined the wall, and books on the mantelpiece. It was quite plain that Mr Smellie was a very learned man!

Larry began to hunt for the shoes he hoped to find. He pulled out a few books from each shelf in the bookcase and ran his hand behind. But there was nothing there. He looked under the piles of paper everywhere but he found no shoes.

Fatty was outside in the hall, keeping guard. He saw the hall cupboard where Daisy had found the shoe, and he thought it would be a good idea to peep into it. Daisy might possibly have overlooked some shoes that might be the right ones. He slipped into the cupboard.

He was so very busy turning up the shoes and boots in the cupboard that he didn't hear someone slipping a latchkey into the front door. He didn't hear someone coming into the hall and quietly closing the front door. So he had no time at all to warn poor Larry to escape! He only heard Mr Smellie when the old man walked into the study and switched on the light!

It was too late to do anything then, of course!

Larry was caught with his head inside a cupboard, not knowing that anyone was in the room until the light was suddenly switched on!

He took his head out of the cupboard in horror. He and Mr Smellie stared at one another, Larry in fright, and Mr Smellie in anger and amazement.

'Robber!' said Mr Smellie angrily. 'Thief! Wicked boy! I'll lock you up and call the police!'

He pounced on Larry and took hold of him with a surprisingly strong hand. Larry gasped. 'Please, sir,' he began, 'please, sir.'

But Mr Smellie was not going to listen to anything. His precious papers were all the world to him, and the sight of somebody rummaging through them filled him with such fury that he was unable to listen to a word. Muttering all sorts of terrible threats, he pushed the boy before him into the hall. Poor Fatty, overcome with shame at having failed to warn Larry, shivered in the hall cupboard outside, not daring to show himself.

'Bad, wicked boy!' he heard Mr Smellie say as he pushed poor Larry up the stairs. Larry was protesting all the time, but Mr Smellie wouldn't listen to a word. 'I'll fetch the police in. I'll hand you over!'

Fatty trembled. It was bad enough to be caught, but it was even worse to think that poor Larry might be handed over to that horrid old Clear-Orf. He heard Mr Smellie take Larry to a room upstairs and lock him in. Miss Miggle, amazed at the sudden noise, came rushing into the hall to see what the matter was.

'Thieves and robbers!' cried Mr Smellie. 'That's what the matter is! I came home just now, walked into my study – and there I found thieves and robbers after my papers!'

Miss Miggle imagined that there must have been two or three men there, and she gaped in astonishment.

'Where are the robbers?' she asked.

'Locked in the boxroom upstairs,' said Mr Smellie. Miss Miggle stared at Mr Smellie in even greater surprise. She couldn't believe that he had taken two or three men upstairs by himself and locked them into the boxroom.

She saw that Mr Smellie was trembling with excitement and shock. 'Now you just go and sit down quietly before you telephone the police,' she said soothingly. 'You're all of a shake! I'll just bring you something to drink. The robbers are safe enough upstairs for a bit.'

Mr Smellie sank down on a chair in the hall. His heart was thumping, and he was breathing hard. 'Be all right in a minute,' he gasped. 'Ha! I got the best of the robbers!'

Miss Miggle ran to the kitchen. Fatty listened breathlessly. Somehow he felt certain that old Mr Smellie had gone back into the study. He didn't know that he was sitting on a chair just at the foot of the stairs.

I'd better take this chance of rescuing poor Larry, thought Fatty, in desperation. He opened the cupboard door and made a dart for the stairs. Mr Smellie was most amazed to see another boy appearing, this time out of the hall cupboard. He could hardly believe his eyes. Was his house alive with boys that night?

He made a grab at Fatty. Fatty was startled and let out a yell. He tried to run up the stairs, and dragged Mr Smellie behind him for a few steps. The old man had got his strength back again by now, and, filled with anger at the sight of what he thought was yet another thief, he clung to

Fatty like a limpet. The boy went up a few more steps, with Mr Smellie almost tearing the coat off his back.

Then Fatty stumbled and sat down heavily on a stair about halfway to the top of the flight. Mr Smellie fell on top of him, almost squashing the boy flat.

'Ow-wow!' yelled poor Fatty. 'Get off! You're hurting me!'

Miss Miggle dropped the glass she was holding and rushed into the hall. What in the wide world could be going on? Was the whole house full of robbers? She was just in time to see Fatty wriggle out from under Mr Smellie and roll down the stairs to the bottom, with many bumps and loud groans.

She saw at once that he was only a boy, and she spoke to him severely.

'What's the meaning of this? How dare you come into someone else's house? What's your name and where do you live?'

Fatty decided to be very upset and hurt. Miss Miggle was a very kind soul, and perhaps she would let him off if she thought he was nothing but a bad little boy out on an escapade.

So Fatty lifted up his voice and howled. Larry heard him, and wondered whatever could be happening. He banged at the locked door, adding to the noise and commotion. Miss Miggle looked quite bewildered.

'He's locked my friend into a room upstairs,' howled Fatty. 'I was just going up to rescue him when Mr Smellie caught me and threw me down the stairs. Oh, I'm covered with bruises! What my mother will say when she sees them I really don't know. She'll have Mr Smellie up for injuring a child! She'll call in the police!'

'Now you can't possibly be bruised yet,' said Miss Miggle. 'I'm sure such a kind old man as Mr Smellie wouldn't hit you, and he wouldn't throw you down the stairs. Don't be a naughty little storyteller!'

'I'm not, I'm not!' said Fatty, pretending to weep.

To Miss Miggle's extreme astonishment and to Mr Smellie's horror, the boy in the hall had several bruises. It did not occur to either of them that the boy had had them for one or two days already.

'Mr Smellie!' said Miss Miggle, 'Just look at this boy's bruises! How could you do that to a little boy? What his parents will say I really do not dare to think.'

Mr Smellie was simply horrified when he thought that he had been the cause of Fatty's awful bruises. He swallowed hard once or twice, and stared at Fatty. 'Better put something on the bruises,' he suggested at last.

'I'll do that whilst you phone for the police,' said Miss Miggle, remembering the other robbers whom she still supposed were locked up in the boxroom above.

But Mr Smellie didn't seem to want to phone for the police now. He looked a bit sheepish, and said, 'Well, Miss Miggle, perhaps it would be better to ask the boys for an explanation of their curious behaviour in my house before I call in the police.'

'Will you let my friend out, please?' said Fatty. 'We didn't come here to rob you. It was only a joke, really. Let's call it quits, shall we? If you don't say anything to the police, we won't tell our mothers – and I won't show my bruises.'

Mr Smellie cleared his throat. Miss Miggle looked at him. 'So the robbers and thieves were only two small boys!' she said. 'Dear, dear! Why didn't you call *me*? I could have settled the matter without all this noise and commotion and throwing down the stairs!'

'I didn't throw him down the stairs,' said Mr Smellie, going up to let Larry out of the boxroom. Very soon Larry was down in the hall with Fatty, and Mr Smellie took them both into his study. Miss Miggle came in with some stuff to put on Fatty's bruises. Larry looked most astonished but didn't say a word.

'Dear, dear, I never in my life saw such dreadful bruises on any child!' said Miss Miggle, dabbing each bruise with the stuff from her bottle.

'What were you two boys doing in my house tonight?' said Mr Smellie sharply. Larry and Fatty were silent. They really didn't know what to say.

'You'll have to tell him that,' said Miss Miggle. 'You didn't come in here for any good purpose, I'll be bound. Now be good boys and own up.'

Still the boys were silent. Mr Smellie suddenly lost his temper. 'Unless you tell me what you came here for I *will* hand you over to the police!' he said.

'Well, I don't know what they'll say when they see all my bruises,' said Fatty.

'I've an idea those bruises were made before tonight!' said Mr Smellie, getting sharper and sharper. 'I know what yellow means in a bruise, if Miss Miggle doesn't!'

The boys said nothing. 'Names and addresses?' barked Mr Smellie, getting out a pen. 'I'll see your parents as well as the police.'

The idea of their fathers and mothers knowing that they had been caught wandering about someone else's house at night was much more alarming than having in the police. Larry suddenly surrendered.

'We came to bring back a shoe we took this morning,' he said in a low voice. Both Miss Miggle and Mr Smellie stared as if they thought Larry had gone mad.

'A *shoe*?' said Mr Smellie at last. 'Why a shoe? And why only *one*? What are you talking about?'

'We were looking for a shoe that fitted a footprint,' said Larry desperately.

This was even more puzzling to the two listeners. Mr Smellie tapped his pen impatiently on his desk. 'Explain properly,' he said. 'I give you one minute. At the end of that time I telephone the police and also your parents, if you haven't given me a full and proper explanation of your most extraordinary conduct.'

'It's no use,' said Fatty to Larry. 'We'll have to tell him the real reason, even if it does warn him and put him on his guard.'

'What *are* you talking about?' said Miss Miggle, who was getting more and more astonished.

'Put me on my guard!' said Mr Smellie. 'What do you mean? Really, I begin to think that you two boys are completely mad.'

'We're not,' said Larry sulkily. 'But we happen to know something about you, Mr Smellie. We know that you were in Mr Hick's house on the evening of the fire.'

The effect of these words was most astonishing. Mr Smellie dropped his pen on the floor and sprang to his feet. His glasses fell off his nose, and his beard shook and quivered. Miss Miggle also looked immensely surprised.

'You *were* there, weren't you?' said Larry. 'Somebody saw you. They told us.'

'Who told you?' spluttered Mr Smellie.

'Horace Peeks saw you,' said Larry. 'He was in the house himself that evening, getting some of his things before Mr Hick came back – and he saw you. How will you explain that to the police?'

'Oh, Mr Smellie, sir, what were you doing down there that evening?' cried poor Miss Miggle, at once thinking that her employer might possibly have set fire to the cottage.

Mr Smellie sat down and put his glasses on his nose again. 'Miss Miggle,' he said, 'I see that you suspect me of setting fire to Mr Hick's workroom. How you can think such a thing after serving me all these years, and knowing that I cannot even kill a fly, I don't know!'

'Well, why did you go there, then?' asked Miss Miggle. 'You'd better tell me, sir. I'll look after you, whatever you've done!'

'I don't need any looking after,' said Mr Smellie, with some sharpness. 'All I went down to Mr Hick's for was to get the papers I had forgotten to bring away with me after my quarrel with the fellow that morning. I certainly went into his house – but I did not go near the

168

workroom. I got my papers – and here they are on the table. I showed them to this boy and his sister this very morning!'

16. SURPRISES AND SHOCKS

All three stared at Mr Smellie, who was quite clearly speaking the truth.

'Golly!' said Larry. 'So that's why you went there. Didn't you hide in the ditch, then?'

'No, of course not,' said Mr Smellie. 'I walked down the drive quite openly, found the garden door open and went in and collected my papers. Then I walked out. I hid nowhere – unless you think that standing by the gate for a little while, to make sure no one was about, was hiding.'

'Oh,' said Larry. This was terribly puzzling. If what Mr Smellie said was true, then there were no suspects left at all. But *some*body must have done the deed!

'And now will you kindly tell me what you took my shoe for?' asked Mr Smellie.

Larry told him, and then Fatty told him who had now got the shoe. Mr Smellie was annoyed.

'That interfering policeman!' he said. 'He has been up and down past my house goodness knows how many times today. I suppose he has been suspecting me too. Now he's got my shoe. I do think you boys deserve punishment.'

'Well, sir, we are only trying to find out who started the fire,' said Fatty. He told Mr Smellie all they had done so far. Miss Miggle listened in admiration and amazement. She was divided between indignation that the boys should have suspected Mr Smellie so strongly, and astonishment that they should have found so many clues and suspects.

'Well,' said Mr Smellie at last. 'I think it's about time you went home, you two. I can assure you that I had nothing whatever to do with the fire, and have no idea who had. I shouldn't think it would be Horace Peeks. More likely the old tramp. Anyway, my advice to you is to leave it to the police. You children will never find out things like that.'

The boys stood up. 'Sorry about your shoe, sir,' said Fatty.

'So am I,' said Mr Smellie dryly. 'It's got my

name inside. So I've no doubt Mr Goon will be along here in the morning. Goodnight. And try not to suspect me of any more fires, thefts, killings, or anything of that sort, will you? I am really only a harmless elderly fellow interested in nothing but my old papers!'

The boys left, distinctly subdued. They couldn't help thinking that Mr Smellie hadn't had anything to do with the burning of the cottage. But, then, who had?

'I'm tired,' said Larry. 'Meet tomorrow at Pip's place. Your bruises came in useful, Fatty. Without them I don't believe we'd have got free!'

'They looked fine, didn't they?' said Fatty cheerfully. 'Well, goodnight. We've had an adventurous evening, haven't we?'

The other three were amazed and admiring when they heard all that had happened to Larry and Fatty. But they were even more puzzled than amazed.

'It's a most extraordinary thing,' said Pip thoughtfully. 'We keep finding that all kinds of people were hiding in the garden that night – and all of them were there for some definite reason. Even the tramp – he was after eggs. And yet we can't put our fingers on the real wrong-doer. *Could* the tramp have done it? *Could* Horace have set fire to the cottage, although he was only gone three minutes? *Could* Mr Smellie have done it? Horace says he saw him in the house, getting his papers – but it's possible he might have burnt the cottage after that.'

'Yes. But somehow I feel certain he didn't now,' said Larry. 'Let's go down to Hiccup's garden and have a big think. We may have missed something.'

They all went down. They saw Lily hanging out the clothes, and whistled to her. With a quick look round to see that Mrs Minns was not about, she ran to them.

'Lily! Where exactly did you and Horace hide in the bushes?' asked Larry. 'Were you in the ditch by the workroom?'

'Oh no,' said Lily, and she pointed to some bushes by the drive. 'We were there. We never went near the ditch.'

'And old Smellie says he only hid for a moment by the gate. But *some*one hid in the ditch!' said Fatty thoughtfully. 'Let's go there, everyone.'

They went to the ditch. The nettles were rising

up again by this time, but it was still easy to see where they had been flattened by someone. The children squeezed through the gap and went to look at the footprint on the space where the turf had been taken away. It was still there, but fainter now.

'You know,' said Daisy suddenly, 'you know, these footprints – the one here and the ones round about the stile – all point one way. They are coming towards the house, but not going away. Whoever hid in the ditch came across the fields to the house – but there are no footprints at all to show that he went back that way.'

'He might have gone out of the front gate, silly,' said Fatty. 'Well, I must say I feel defeated today. Our clues don't tell us anything now – and all our suspects seem to be innocent. I feel a bit tired of finding out things that lead us nowhere. Let's do something else today. Let's go for an all-day picnic.'

'Oooh *yes*,' said everyone. 'We'll go back for our bikes. We'll go to Burnham Beeches and have a lovely time.'

Bets' mother would not allow her to go, because

it was too far for an eight year old to ride. The little girl was very disappointed.

'I'd rather Bets didn't go for a picnic today anyway,' said her mother. 'She looks a bit pale. Leave Buster behind and let her go for a walk with him. She'll like that.'

Bets did love taking Buster for walks, but it hardly made up for missing a picnic. Fatty was very sorry for her when she stood at the gate waving to them as they went off on their bikes.

'I'll bring you back heaps of primroses!' he called. 'Look after Buster, won't you?'

Buster wagged his tail. He meant to look after Bets, not have Bets look after *him*! He too felt sad when he saw the children going off without him. But he knew that he could never run fast enough to keep up with bicycles.

It had been raining in the night and everywhere was muddy. Bets thought she had better put on her rubber boots. She went to get them. Buster pattered after her on muddy paws.

'It's a pity *you* can't wear boots or something, Buster,' she said. 'You get awfully muddy.'

The two of them set off for a walk. Bets went

down the lane to the river. She chose a little path that ran alongside the river for some way, and then turned back again across a field that led to the stile where the children had seen the exciting footprints a few days before.

Bets danced along, throwing sticks for Buster, and remembering not to throw stones for him to fetch because Fatty said they broke his teeth. She stooped down to pick up a stick – and then stood still in the greatest astonishment.

There, plainly to be seen on the muddy path in front of her, was a line of footprints exactly like the ones the children had found by the stile! Bets by now knew the prints by heart, for she had gazed at Fatty's drawings so often. She felt absolutely certain that they were the same. There was the rubber sole with its criss-cross markings, and the little squares with the blobs at each corner!

'Ooh, look, Buster,' said Bets at last. She could feel her heart thumping with excitement. Buster came to look. He sniffed at the footprints and then looked up at Bets, wagging his tail.

'They're the same prints, aren't they, Buster, dear?' said Bets. 'And listen, Buster – it only rained last night – so someone must have walked along here since then – and that someone is the person we're after – though we don't know who! Oh, Buster – what's the best thing to do? I do feel so excited, don't you?'

Buster capered round the little girl as if he understood every single word she said. She stood for a moment or two looking down at the line of footprints.

'We'll follow them, Buster,' she said. 'That's what we'll do! We'll follow them. See? I don't know how long it is since the person walked along here, but it's not very long, anyway. Come on – we may even catch up with the person who made the prints. Oh, this *is* exciting!'

The little girl followed the footprints with Buster. He put his nose down to them and followed them too, though it was really the smell he was following, not the marks themselves. Along the muddy path they went, and then crossed a road to the other side. Then up another footpath, where they showed quite plainly, and then into a lane. Here they were not so easy to follow, but Buster's nose was most useful, for he could follow the smell, even where there was no footprint to be seen.

'You really are very clever, Buster,' said Bets, in great admiration. 'I wish my nose was like yours, Yes – that's right – that's another of the prints – and here's another – and another. Look – they're going to the stile.'

So they were. It was plain that the owner of the prints had crossed the stile and jumped down on to the field beyond. Bets grew more and more excited.

'The prints are going the same way as the other prints did!' she said to Buster. 'Look! Now, Buster, dear, use your nose well across this field because I can't see anything on the grass, of course.'

Buster went across the field in a straight line, his black nose held close to the ground. He could smell exactly where the person had walked. Soon Bets came to a bare muddy bit and there she saw a footprint clearly outlined. 'You are going the right way, Buster,' she said. 'Keep your nose down! Hurry! Maybe we shall find the person if we're quick! I believe these footprints have only just been made.'

The footprints did not lead to the gap in the hedge. Instead they led over another stile and up the lane that led to Bets's own house. But at Mr Hick's gate the prints turned and went up Mr Hick's own drive!

Bets was amazed. So the man who burnt the cottage had actually gone back to it today! She wondered if he had gone to the front door or the back door. She went up the muddy drive, her face down, watching the prints. They went right to the front door. Just as she got there the door opened and Mr Hick appeared. He seemed astonished to see Bets.

'Well, what are *you* doing here?' he asked.

'Oh, Mr Hick,' gasped Bets, too excited to think that she might be giving away any of the Find-Outers' secrets. 'I'm following these footprints, and they go right to your door. Oh, Mr Hick, it's most awfully important to know who made them. Has anyone been to see you today?'

Mr Hick looked surprised, and he frowned at Bets and Buster. 'I don't understand,' he said. 'Why is it so awfully important?'

'Well, if only I knew who made these footprints I should be able to tell the others who set fire to your cottage the other evening,' said Bets importantly.

Mr Hick looked completely bewildered, and he stared very hard indeed at Bets. 'You'd better come in,' he said at last. 'This is very extraordinary. What is a child like you doing, following footprints – and how do you know anything about it? Come in. No – leave the dog outside.'

'Let him come too,' said Bets. 'He'll be very, very good. He'll scratch your door down if you leave him outside.'

So Buster went in too, and soon the three of them were sitting in Mr Hick's study, which, like Mr Smellie's, was littered with papers and books.

'Now,' said Mr Hick, trying to speak in a pleasant voice, which was very difficult for him. 'Now, little girl, you tell me why you followed those footprints and what you know about them. It may be a help to me.'

Bets, proud to have a grown-up listening to her so closely, poured out the whole story of the Find-Outers and what they had done. She told Mr Hick about the clues and the suspects, and he listened without saying a single word.

Buster made himself a perfect nuisance all the time. He would keep going over to Mr Hick, sniffing at him, and trying to nibble his feet. Mr Hick got most annoyed, but Buster wouldn't leave him alone. In the end Bets had to take him on her knee and keep him there.

When she had finished her story, right up to that very morning, she looked eagerly at Mr Hick. 'Now will you tell me who came here today?' she asked.

'Well,' said Mr Hick slowly, 'as it happens, two of your suspects came here. Mr Smellie came to borrow a book – and Horace Peeks came to ask me for a reference.'

'Oh! So it might be either of them,' said Bets. 'I do wonder which of them wore the rubber-soled shoes with those markings. Well, anyway, now we know for certain it was one of those two. Mr Hick, you won't tell a single soul what I've told you this morning, will you?'

'Certainly not,' said Mr Hick. 'A lot of people seem to have been in my garden that day I went up to town, didn't they? Wait till I get my fingers on the one who played that dirty trick on me, and burnt all my valuable papers!'

'I'd better go now,' said Bets. She stood up, and

put Buster down. He immediately rushed to Mr Hick and began to sniff at his trousers in a way that Mr Hick thoroughly disliked.

'You go now and take that dog with you,' said Mr Hick. 'And my advice to you children is – don't meddle in things that concern grown-ups. Leave the police to do the finding-out!'

'Oh, we *must* go on,' said Bets. 'After all, we *are* the Find-Outers!'

She went up the drive with Buster and saw the footprints once again. One row went up the drive and one row went down. How Bets wished she knew whether the prints had been made by Mr Smellie or Mr Peeks! She longed and longed for the others to come home. She could hardly wait to tell them her news. She wondered if they would mind her telling Mr Hick all that she had told him. But, after all, it couldn't matter *him* knowing. He would do all he could to help them, Bets was sure – and he had faithfully promised not to tell anyone at all.

The others came back after tea, tired and happy after a lovely day at Burnham Beeches. Fatty presented Bets with an enormous bunch of primroses.

Bets could not wait for one moment to tell them her news. She was simply bursting with it – but just as she was in the middle of it, there came a very nasty surprise!

Up the garden appeared Pip's mother, and with her was Clear-Orf, looking very smug and also very forbidding.

'Old Clear-Orf!' said Larry, in a low tone. 'Whatever does he want?'

It was soon quite clear what he had come for! Pip's mother spoke to the children in a very stern voice.

'Children! Mr Goon has come to me with a very extraordinary story of your doings in the last few days. I can hardly believe what he says!'

'What's the matter?' asked Pip, scowling at Clear-Orf.

'Pip, don't scowl like that,' said his mother sharply. 'Apparently all of you have been inter-fering in matters that concern the police. Even Bets! I simply cannot understand it. Mr Goon even tells me that you and Frederick, Larry, got into Mr Smellie's house last night. What *will* your mothers say? And even little Bets has been following footprints and imagining herself to be a detective!'

'Who told Mr Goon that?' burst out Bets. 'Nobody knows but me – and Mr Hick!'

'Mr Hick rang me up, and I have just been to see him,' said Mr Goon, speaking with great dignity. 'He told me all your goings-on – interfering little busybodies!'

Bets burst into loud sobs. 'Oh, Mr Hick told me he wouldn't tell *any*one!' she wailed. 'Oh, he did promise me faithfully! He's a wicked, wicked man! He's broken his faithful promise. I hate him!'

'Bets! Behave yourself!' said her mother.

'Of course, Bets *would* go and give everything away!' said Pip sulkily. That's what comes of having her in the Find-Outers. Little idiot! She goes and tells everything to Mr Hick, he rings up Clear-Orf, and now we're all in the soup!'

'What are you muttering about, Pip?' said his mother. 'Who is Clear-Orf?'

'Mr Goon,' said Pip defiantly. 'He's always telling us to clear orf.'

'Ho!' said Mr Goon, swelling himself out like an angry frog, his blue eyes bulging fiercely. 'Ho! Didn't I always find you hanging about, you kids?

Regular pests you are. Now you just listen to me for a few minutes.'

There was absolutely nothing to be done but listen to Mr Goon. The five children stood there, red and angry, Bets still sobbing. Only Buster didn't seem to care, but sniffed happily round Clear-Orf, who fended him off every now and again.

Clear-Orf had a lot to say about 'nosey children' and 'little nuisances' and 'interfering with the law.' He ended up with a threat.

'And if I come across any of you nosing about again, or if Mr Hick reports you to me, you'll all get into very serious trouble,' he said. 'Ho yes – VERY SERIOUS TROUBLE. You keep out of matters that don't concern you. And as for you, Laurence and Daisy, and you Frederick, *your* parents are going to hear about this as well. You mark my words, you'll be sorry you ever interfered with the law.'

'We didn't,' said Pip desperately. 'We only tried to help.'

'Now, no backchat!' said Mr Goon majestically. 'Children can't help in these things. They only get into trouble – very serious trouble.'

And with that Mr Goon departed with Pip's mother, a burly, righteous-looking figure in dark blue.

17. VERY STRANGE DISCOVERIES

A storm of anger broke over poor Bets when Mr Goon had gone.

'Idiot!' said Pip. 'Going and blabbing everything out to old Hiccup!'

'Honestly, you've ruined everything, Bets,' said Daisy.

'This is the end of the Find-Outers,' said Larry gloomily. 'That's what comes of having a baby in it like Bets. Everything's spoilt.'

Bets sobbed loudly. Fatty was sorry for her. He actually put his arm round her and spoke kindly, though he felt as impatient as the others at the break-up of their plans and hopes.

'Don't cry, Bets. We all do silly things. It was clever of you and Buster to track those prints, I must say. And wouldn't I like to know which of those two, Mr Peeks or Mr Smellie, wore those shoes!'

Pip's mother appeared again, looking stern. 'I

hope you are feeling ashamed of yourselves,' she said. 'I want you all to go down and apologise to Mr Hick for interfering in his concerns. He is naturally very annoyed to think that you have been messing about each day in his garden.'

'We didn't do any harm,' said Pip.

'That's not the point,' said his mother. 'You children simply *can*not be allowed to go on to private property, and into private houses without permission. You will all go down immediately to Mr Hick and apologise. Do as I say at once.'

The children set off together down the drive, with Buster at their heels. They were all sulky and mutinous. They hated having to apologise to someone they detested. Also they all felt that it was terribly mean of Mr Hick to have given Bets away like that, when he had solemnly promised not to.

'He's a nasty piece of work,' said Larry, and everyone agreed.

'I don't care *who* set fire to his workroom,' said Fatty. 'I'm glad it *was* burnt down, and his precious papers too.'

'You shouldn't say things like that,' said

Daisy, though she felt much the same herself at that moment.

They arrived at the house and rang the bell. Bets pointed out the footprints and they all gazed at them with interest. Bets was right. The prints were exactly like the ones in Fatty's drawing. It was too bad that they had to give up the search for the criminal just as they had almost found the man!

Mrs Minns opened the door and was surprised to see the little company. Sweetie, who was at her heels, fled away with tail up in the air as soon as she saw Buster.

'Please, will you tell Mr Hiccup – er, I mean Mr Hick – that we want to see him?' said Larry. Mrs Minns looked even more surprised, and was about to answer when a voice called from the study.

'Who's that, Mrs Minns?'

'Five children and a dog, sir,' answered Mrs Minns. 'They say they want to see you.'

There was a pause. 'Bring them in,' said Mr Hick's voice, and very solemnly the children and Buster went into the study. Mr Hick was there, sitting in a big chair, his legs crossed, and his crest of hair looking rather alarming.

'What have you come for?' he asked.

'Mother said we were all to apologise to you, Mr Hick,' said Pip. And, with one voice, the children chanted in a most mournful tone, 'We apologise, Mr Hick!'

'Hmmm,' said Mr Hick, looking more amiable. 'I should think so, indeed!'

'You said you wouldn't tell anyone,' burst out Bets. 'You broke your promise.'

Mr Hick didn't consider that promises made to children need be kept at all, so he didn't feel guilty or say he was sorry. He was about to say something when several aeroplanes passed over the garden, rather low. The noise made him jump and Buster growled. Larry ran to the window. He was extremely good at spotting any kind of aeroplane that flew overhead.

'It's those jets again!' he cried. 'I've only seen them twice over here. Look at their curious tail-fins.'

'They were over here two or three days ago,' said Mr Hick, with interest. 'I saw them. There were seven. Are there seven today?'

Larry counted them. All the children looked out

of the window – except Fatty. He didn't look out of the window. He looked at Mr Hick with a most bewildered expression on his face. He opened his mouth as if to speak, and then firmly closed it again. But he still went on staring at Mr Hick, very deep in thought.

The jets came over again, roaring low. 'Let's go out and see them,' said Larry. 'We can see them better outdoors. Good-bye, Mr Hick.'

'Good-bye. And don't poke and pry again into matters that don't concern children,' said Mr Hick stiffly. 'It was probably Horace Peeks that fired my workroom. The police will soon make out a case against him. He wore rubber-soled shoes this morning when he came to see me, and there is no doubt that he made those prints up and down the drive.'

'Oh,' said the children, feeling very sorry for poor Lily. She would be terribly upset they knew. Only Fatty said nothing, but looked hard at Mr Hick again, a curious expression on his face. They all went out – but the jets were now gone again, leaving a faint throbbing behind them.

'Well, that's done,' said Larry, with relief. 'How

I hated apologising to that mean fellow! I suppose Mr Peeks did do it, after all – burnt the cottage, I mean.'

Fatty was very silent as they all walked down the lane towards the river. They meant to go for a short walk before suppertime. Bets looked at Fatty.

'What's the matter?' she asked.

'I was thinking of something very, very, very odd!' said Fatty.

'What was it?' asked the others, interested. Fatty stopped and pointed up into the sky. 'You know those planes we saw?' he said. The others nodded.

'Well,' said Fatty, 'they were jets, and they have only been over here twice – once today – and once on the evening of the day that the cottage was burnt!'

'Well – what about it?' said Larry impatiently. 'Nothing odd about that, surely!'

'Listen,' said Fatty, 'when we spoke about those jets, what did Mr Hick say? He said that he saw them when they were over here two or three days ago – and he counted them and there were seven. Which was quite correct.'

'What are you getting at?' asked Pip, frowning.

'I'm getting at something peculiar,' said Fatty. 'Where was Mr Hick on the evening that the fire was started?'

'On the London train!' said Larry.

'Then how could he have seen and counted the jets that flew over *here*?' said Fatty.

There was a startled silence. Everyone thought hard. Larry spoke first. 'It *is* peculiar!' he said. 'Those planes *have* only been here twice – everyone spoke about them. And if Hiccup saw them that evening – then he must have been *here*!'

'And yet his chauffeur met the London train and he walked off it!' said Daisy. 'He couldn't possibly have seen the planes if he was really on the train, because at that time the train had hardly started out from London!'

'And so,' said Fatty, a note of triumph in his voice, 'and so, Find-Outers, we have yet another suspect. Mr Hick himself!'

'Oooh,' said Bets, amazed. 'But he wouldn't burn his own cottage!'

'He might – to get the insurance money on his valuable papers,' said Fatty. 'People do do that sometimes. I expect he sold the papers – then set fire to the workroom and pretended the papers were burnt, in order to get more money. Golly! Can it really be possible?'

'We can't tell anyone,' said Daisy.

'I should think not!' said Larry. 'Whatever in the world shall we do about it?'

'We must find out how it was that Mr Hick got on the London train that night,' said Fatty. 'Look – we're near the railway line here. The London trains always come by here, and there's one due. Let's see what happens.'

The children climbed on to the fence by the railway and sat there, waiting. Soon they saw a train in the distance. It came roaring along – but when it reached one portion of the line, it slowed down, and finally it stopped.

'It always stops there,' said Bets. 'I've noticed that. Perhaps there's a signal or something.'

It was too far away to see why it had stopped. Anyway it soon started up again, and rushed by the five children. Buster ran away behind a bush when it came. He was afraid of the noise.

Fatty was again thinking very deeply. So was Larry. 'Listen,' said Fatty. 'Is it possible for anyone at night to wait for the train just there, and hop into an empty carriage, do you think? Then, at Peterswood Station, if he had a season ticket, people would never know he hadn't come all the way from London.'

'Fatty, I believe you're right!' said Larry. 'I was just thinking the very same thing myself. I believe Hiccup could have done it. Pretended to go to London – slipped back – hid in the ditch, leaving those few footprints behind him – set fire to the cottage – slipped back to the railway line just there – waited till the train stopped, as it always does – hopped into an empty carriage in the dark – and then got out as cool as a cucumber, to be met by his car and chauffeur at the station!'

The more the children thought about this, the more certain they felt that Mr Hick might have done it. 'After all,' said Bets, 'a man that could break his faithful promise could do *any*thing, simply *any*thing.'

'Whatever is Buster doing?' said Fatty, hearing some excited barks coming from the little dog, some way back in the copse of trees behind them. 'Buster! BUSTER! What's the matter? Found a rabbit?'

Buster yelped and then appeared, dragging something black and muddy. 'Whatever *has* he got?' said Bets.

Everyone looked to see. 'It's an old shoe!' said Daisy, laughing. 'Buster, what do you want with an old shoe?'

Buster went to Bets and laid the shoe down at her feet. Then he stood looking up at her, as if he was telling her something, wagging his tail hard. Bets picked up the shoe. She turned it over.

'*Look*!' said Bets. 'The real proper shoe at last! The one that made the footprints!'

The others nearly fell off the fence in their excitement. Bets was perfectly right. It was THE SHOE!

'Buster followed the footprints and knew their smell, and when he smelt the shoe hidden over there he knew the smell again, and that's why he brought it to *me*,' cried Bets. 'We had followed the prints together, you see. Oh, and now I know why he kept on and on sniffing round Mr Hick's shoes when I went to see him. He could smell the same smell!'

'Clever dog,' said Fatty, patting Buster. 'Where's

the other shoe, old fellow? Find it, find it!'

Buster rushed off to a bush not far away and began to scrape violently beneath it. Soon he unearthed the other shoe and laid it at Fatty's feet. The children picked it up.

'Well!' said Fatty. 'This is very strange. I suppose old Hiccup got the wind up after Bets had told him she had followed the footprints, and went out and buried the shoes in case the police should find them in his house, or spot him wearing them. And good old Buster smelt them out. Clever, good, marvellous dog! Big bone for you tomorrow, Buster, a GREAT BIG BONE!'

'And now – whatever are we going to do about everything?' said Larry, going back to the path. 'It's no good telling the police. We're in disgrace and wouldn't be listened to. It's no good telling our parents. We're in enough trouble as it is.'

'Let's go and sit down by the river and talk about it,' said Pip. 'Come on. We'll simply *have* to decide something. Things are getting very serious.'

18. AN UNEXPECTED FRIEND

The children made their way along the path that led to the river. They found a sheltered place on the high bank of the river and sat down. Buster growled a little but sat down with them.

'What are you growling for, Buster?' said Bets. 'Don't you want to sit down?'

Buster growled again and then stopped. The children began to talk.

'It's a funny thing,' said Pip, 'we've found the man who started the fire – and we've got all the facts – we know how he got on to the London train – we know that his shoes fit the footprints – we know that he was afraid and hid those shoes – which we've found – and we know why all the other suspects were down in the garden that evening. We know everything – and yet we can't do anything about it because Mr Goon would be sure to pretend that *he* found out everything!'

'Yes – it's no good telling the police,' said Fatty gloomily. 'And it's no good telling our parents either, because they would just ring up Mr Goon. Isn't it perfectly sickening to think that we've solved the mystery and found out simply everything, and we can't get the criminal punished. Horrid Mr Hick! He ought to be punished. Don't you think it was mean the way he tried to lay the blame on poor old Mr Peeks when he thought we were getting to know too much?'

'Yes,' agreed every one.

'It was funny the way he gave himself away by mentioning those aeroplanes,' said Larry. 'It was really smart of Fatty to spot that, I think.'

'It certainly was,' said Daisy warmly, and the others nodded.

Fatty swelled up at once. 'Well, as I've told you before,' he said, 'I really *have* got brains. Now, at school . . .'

'Shut up, Fatty,' said everyone together, and Fatty subsided and shut up, still feeling pleased, however, that the others admired him for spotting such a curious clue.

They all went on talking about the burnt cottage

and the suspects and clues for a little while longer, and then Buster growled so fiercely and so long that everyone was surprised and puzzled.

'What *is* the matter with Buster?' said Bets. 'Has he got a tummy-ache or something, do you think?'

She had hardly finished saying these words when a large round face appeared above the rim of the high river bank. It was a kindly face, set with big intelligent eyes that had a real twinkle in them.

'Oh!' said everyone, startled.

'Pardon me,' said the face. 'I'm afraid I've frightened you. But, you see, I was sitting down here, below the bank, in my favourite corner, fishing. Naturally I kept quiet, because I didn't want to disturb the fish. I couldn't help hearing what you were talking about – it was most interesting, *most* interesting, if you'll pardon my saying so!'

Buster barked so loudly that the children could hardly hear what the hidden person was saying. He climbed up on to the bank beside them, and they saw that he was a very big fellow, burly and strong, dressed in a tweed suit and enormous brown shoes.

The man sat down beside them and took out a bar of chocolate, which he broke into bits and offered the children. They couldn't help liking him.

'Did you hear everything we said?' asked Bets. 'It was really all a secret, you know. We're the Find-Outers.'

'The Fine Doubters?' said the man, puzzled. 'What do you doubt then?'

Everyone giggled. 'No – the Finddddd-Outers,' said Daisy, sounding the letter D loudly at the end of 'Find'. 'We find out things.'

'Ah! I see,' said the big man. Buster was now quite friendly towards him and licked his hand. The big man patted him.

'What are you?' asked Bets. 'I haven't seen you before.'

'Well – if you don't mind my saying so – I'm a bit of a Find-Outer myself,' said the man. 'I have to solve mysteries too. Most interesting it is – I'm sure you agree with me?'

'Oh *yes*,' said everyone.

'I gather that you are in a spot of bother at the moment?' said the man. 'You have solved your mystery – but you can't make your discoveries known? Is that right?'

'Yes,' said Larry. 'You see – Mr Goon, the policeman here, doesn't like us, and has complained to our parents about some things we did. Well – I dare say some of them were pretty awful, really – but we did them in a good cause. I mean – we wanted to find out who burnt down Mr Hick's cottage.'

'And now that you have found out, you have got to keep quiet about it,' said the man. 'Most annoying for you. Tell me more about it. As I say – I'm a bit of a Find-Outer too, in my way – so I enjoy talking over a mystery as man to man, if you see what I mean.'

The children looked at the big, burly fellow on the bank. His keen eyes twinkled at them, and his big hand patted Buster. Larry looked round at the others.

'I think we might as well tell him everything, don't you?' said Larry. They nodded. They all trusted the big fisherman, and somehow knew that their secrets were safe with him.

So Larry, interrupted sometimes by Daisy, Fatty

and Pip, told the whole story of the Find-Outers, and what they had discovered. The big man listened keenly, sometimes putting in a question, nodding his head every now and again.

'Smart boy, you,' he said to Fatty, when Larry came to the bit about how Mr Hick had given himself away by saying that he had seen the seven jets on the evening of the fire. Fatty went red with pleasure, and Bets squeezed his hand.

The story was finished at last. The big man looked round.

'An extremely good piece of work, if I may say so,' he said, beaming round. 'I congratulate the Five Find-Outers – and Dog! And – I think I can help you a bit.'

'How?' asked Larry.

'Well, we must get hold of that tramp again,' said the big man. 'From what you say he said to you, he probably saw Mr Hick in the garden too – hiding in the ditch – and that would be valuable evidence. And er – certainly the police ought to know about all this.'

'Oh,' said everyone in dismay, thinking of Clear-Orf, and how he would say that he himself had found out everything. 'And we could never, never find that tramp again!' said Larry. 'He may be miles and miles away.'

'I'll find him for you all right,' promised the big man.

'And old Clear-Orf – that's Mr Goon, you know – won't listen to a word we say, I'm sure,' said Fatty gloomily.

'I'll see that he does,' said the astonishing man, getting up. 'Leave it to me. Call at your police station tomorrow at ten o'clock, will you? I'll be there, and we'll finish up everything nicely.'

He picked up his rod and put it over his shoulder. 'A most interesting talk,' he said. 'Valuable to both of us, as I hope you will agree.'

He strode off in the evening twilight, and the children watched him go. 'Ten o'clock tomorrow at the police station,' said Fatty, feeling rather uncomfortable. 'Whatever's going to happen there? And how is that man going to find the tramp?'

Nobody knew. Larry looked at his watch, gave a yell and leapt to his feet. 'I say – it's *awfu*lly late. We *shall* get into a row. Come along, quickly.'

They hurried home, with Buster at their heels.

'Good-bye!' they called to one another. 'Ten o'clock tomorrow at the police station. Don't be late!'

19. THE END OF THE MYSTERY

The next morning the Five Find-Outers and their dog arrived punctually at the police station. With them they brought their clues, as the big man had requested. There was Fatty's drawing of the footprints, the bit of grey cloth in the match box, and the rubber-soled shoes that had been scraped up by Buster.

'You know, the only clue that wasn't any use was the bit of grey flannel,' said Larry, opening the box. 'We never found out whose coat it belonged to, did we? And yet it must belong to someone who went through that gap! Perhaps Mr Hick wore a grey suit that night. If so, he hasn't worn it since, because he's always had on dark blue whenever we've seen him.'

They went into the police station feeling a little awed. Mr Goon was there, without his helmet, and also another policeman the children didn't know.

They stared at Mr Goon, expecting him to rise up and say, 'Clear orf!'

But he didn't. He told them to sit down in such polite tones that the children were overcome with astonishment. They sat down. Buster went to inspect the policeman's legs, and Clear-Orf didn't even kick out at him.

'We were to meet someone here,' said Fatty. Clear-Orf nodded.

'He'll be along in a minute,' he said. As he spoke, a small police car drove up, and the children looked round, expecting to see their friend, the big man. But he wasn't in the car.

To their surprise there was someone else in it that they knew. It was the old tramp! He was muttering to himself, and looking rather scared.

'I'm an honest old fellow, I am, and nobody never said I wasn't. I'll tell anything I know, course I will, but I won't do nothing to get meself into trouble, that I won't. I've not done nothing wrong.'

There was a plainclothes policeman in the car with him, besides the driver. Bets was surprised when Larry told her that the man in the dark grey suit was a policeman.

'I thought they never, never wore anything but their uniforms,' she said.

Then another car drove up, driven by an extremely smart-looking man in blue uniform. He wore a peaked cap, and the other policemen saluted him smartly when he heaved himself out of the car. The car was big, but the man was big too!

The children gazed at him – and Bets gave a squeal. 'It's the fisherman! It's the man we saw yesterday! Hello!'

'Hello, there!' said the big man, smiling.

'We've found the tramp, Inspector,' said the plainclothes policeman to the big man. The children looked at one another. So their friend was an Inspector of Police! Golly!

'An inspector is a very, very high-up policeman,' whispered Pip to Bets. 'He's terribly clever. Look at old Clear-Orf. He's trembling like a jelly!'

Clear-Orf was not really trembling, but it was plain that he was quite overcome by the visit of the Inspector to his small police station. His hands shook as he turned over the pages of his notebook.

The Inspector beamed at the children. 'Nice to see you again, if I may say so,' he said. He spoke to

Clear-Orf, making Mr Goon jump. 'You are lucky to have five such smart children in your district, Goon,' he said.

Clear-Orf opened and shut his mouth but said nothing. He didn't want smart children in his district, especially any that were smarter than he was! But he couldn't very well say so to his inspector.

Then the tramp was brought before the Inspector and questioned. He answered willingly enough, once he had been assured that he would only do himself good, not harm, by answering truthfully. The children listened intently.

'Tell us all the people you saw in Mr Hick's garden that night,' said the Inspector.

'Well,' said the tramp. 'There was meself, hiding under a bush near the workroom, not doing no harm to nobody – just taking a rest, like.'

'Quite,' said the Inspector.

'Then I saw that fellow who got the sack that morning,' said the tramp. 'Peeks, his name was. He was hiding in the bushes, along with someone else I couldn't see. But by the voice I reckoned it was a girl. Well, I see him going into the house and out again, through a window.'

'Ah,' said the Inspector.

'Then I see an old fellow,' said the tramp. 'I heard him having a quarrel with Mr Hick that day – name of Smellie, wasn't it? Yes. Well, he came walking down the drive, quiet-like, and he slipped into the house by a door, just before Peeks came out again.'

'Go on,' said the Inspector. 'Did you see anyone else?'

'Yes, I did,' said the tramp. 'I see Mr Hick himself!'

Everyone listened breathlessly. 'I was lying under that there bush,' said the tramp, 'thinking that there was a lot of people in the garden that evening, when I heard someone squeezing through the gap in the hedge, not far from me. I looked through the sprays of the bush and I saw it was Mr Hick himself. He stood there in that ditch for a long time, and then he went to a big clump of blackberries and fished up a tin out of the middle where it was hidden.'

Fatty gave a little whistle. It was extraordinary to hear the tramp relating the whole story that they had so carefully pieced together. That tin must have contained petrol!

'Then Mr Hick went to the little cottage nearby, stayed there a while, came out and locked the door, and hid in the ditch again,' said the tramp. 'I lay under my bush as still as a mouse. After a time, when it was really dark, I heard Mr Hick getting out of the ditch and going down the lane towards the railway. Then I saw a light in the cottage and I guessed it was on fire, and I went off mighty quick. I didn't want to be found there and accused of starting it.'

'Thank you,' said the Inspector. 'Was there anyone else at all that you saw?'

'Not a soul,' said the tramp.

'A very pretty plot,' said the Inspector. 'Mr Hick wants money. He manages to pick a quarrel with a good many people that day, so that if by chance the insurance company suspect foul play, there are many people who have reason to burn his cottage out of spite. He gets his chauffeur to take him to the station in the afternoon, to catch the train to town. He must have got out at the next station, and walked back over the fields to his garden, where he hid until he set fire to the cottage. Then he walked back to the railway, waited at the place where the London train always halts for a minute, and gets into an empty carriage, unseen in the darkness. He arrives at Peterswood Station, is met by his chauffeur and driven home, to be told that his workroom is on fire. Very pretty indeed.'

'And now, I think, we must ask Mr Hick a few questions,' said the plainclothes man.

'That is so,' agreed the Inspector. He turned to the children. 'We will let you know what happens,' he said. 'And, if I may say so, I am very proud to have met the Five Find-Outers – and Dog. I trust that we shall work together on other mysteries in the future. I should be extremely grateful for your help – and I am sure Mr Goon feels the same as I do.'

Mr Goon didn't at all, but he could do nothing but nod and try to smile. He was angry to think that the five 'pests' had actually solved the mystery before he had, and that the Inspector was praising them.

'Good-day, Goon,' said the Inspector pleasantly, walking out to his car.

'Good-day, Inspector Jenks,' said poor Clear-Orf.

'Can I give you children a lift?' inquired the Inspector. 'Am I going your way?'

He was, for he was going to Mr Hick with the plainclothes man. The children piled into the big car, bursting with importance, and hoping that everyone in the village would see them riding with their friend, the great Inspector!

'I suppose you couldn't possibly put in a word for us with our parents, could you?' asked Pip. 'You see, Mr Goon complained so bitterly of us. If you spoke well of us, it would be a great help.'

'It would be a pleasure,' beamed the Inspector, starting up his powerful car. 'I'll call in after I've interviewed Mr Hick.'

He kept his word. He called on Pip's mother later in the day, and very much impressed her with his admiration for the Find-Outers.

'They are very smart children,' he said. 'I am sure you will agree with me. I am proud to know them.'

The children crowded round him eagerly. 'What about Mr Hick? What did he say?'

'I questioned him closely, and let him know that we knew everything and had got his shoes too,' said the Inspector. 'He denied it at first, but when asked to explain how it was that he heard those aeroplanes coming over here at the time when he had vowed he was in London, he broke down and confessed everything. So I am afraid Mr Hick will have to leave his comfortable house and spend some considerable time with the police! He is even now on his way, and poor Mrs Minns is in a most excited state.'

'I expect Lily will be glad that Horace isn't suspected any more,' said Daisy. 'And we'd better go and tell Mr Smellie all about it too, so that he will forgive us for getting into his house and taking his shoe. Will Mr Goon give him back his shoe, Inspector Jenks?'

'It has already been done,' said the big man. 'Well, I must be going. I hope I shall see you again some day. You did very well indeed with your clues and your list of suspects.'

'There was only one clue that wasn't any good,' said Larry, pulling out his match box with the bit of grey flannel in. 'We never found any suspect with a grey flannel coat, and a tiny bit torn out of it.'

'Well, if you don't mind my saying so, I have an

idea that I can explain that clue,' said the big Inspector, looking wise.

'Oh, do tell us,' said Bets.

The Inspector pulled Larry to him, swung him round, and showed the others a tiny tear in his grey flannel jacket, just by the armpit at the back.

'That's where your bit of grey cloth came from!' he said, with a deep chuckle. 'You all got through that gap in the hedge when you went to find footprints, didn't you? And Larry must have caught himself a bit on a prickle – and the boy behind him spotted the bit of grey rag on the twig and thought it was a clue! Good thing you didn't see that Larry's coat was torn, or you might have written *him* down as a suspect too!'

The children laughed. 'However was it that nobody noticed Larry's coat was a bit torn?' said Bets, astonished. 'Well – to think of all the things we found out – and we didn't find that out!'

'Good-bye,' said the Inspector, getting into his car. 'Thanks for your help. It's a very satisfactory ending, as I'm sure you will agree with me!'

'Rather!' said everyone. 'Good-bye! It *was* a bit of luck meeting you!'

The car roared off up the lane. The children turned back into the garden.

'What an exciting week we've had,' said Daisy. 'I suppose now the Find-Outers must come to an end, because we've solved the mystery!'

'No,' said Fatty. 'We'll still be the Five Find-Outers and Dog, because you simply *never* know when another mystery will come along for us to solve. We'll just wait till it comes.'

They are waiting – and one will come, there's no doubt about that.

But, of course, that will be quite another story!

/